BERNARDONE'S KNIGHTS

A Star Crossed Crescent Book III

JC Ernst

Copyright Jan. 2015
Without limiting the rights under copyright reserved above, no part of this publication may be reproduced, stored in or introduced into a retrieval system, or transmitted, in any form, or by any means (electronic, mechanical, photocopying, or otherwise), without the prior written permission of the copyright owner JC Ernst.

Note:

This is a work of fiction. Names, characters, places and incidents either are the product of the author's imagination or are used fictitiously, and any resemblance to actual persons, living or dead, business establishments, events, or locales is strictly coincidental.

Cover Art:
The artwork on the front cover is a combination of original work, as well as a famous piece of work Titled Saint Francis Defeats the Antichrist, by Christibol De Villalpando. The original work composed in the late seventeenth century, is now part of the permanent collection at the Philadelphia Museum of art.

Copyright © 2017 JC Ernst
All rights reserved.

ISBN: 1545347999
ISBN 13: 9781545347997

I want to say a special thank you to Ed Torkelson and Rusty Green for the support and encouragement. You were invaluable in your assistance. I want to thank my wife Sherlene for putting up with all the long preoccupied nights and inattentive days when I was writing. Thanks to all who are out there doing good for nothing more than goodness sake.

PROLOGUE

Near middle of a pile of papers, stacked in a gun safe, in a garage, in Sedona, Arizona was a letter. It was written by Jake Rader to his dad. On first blush it seemed like nothing more than a simple communication; something one might find along with letters from camp, birthday cards and so on. However, this correspondence was different. It was significant.

In part, because it became background material for the article originally published in the Phoenix Sands nearly a year ago. This simple crumpled page with evidence of coffee and water drips is now the source of international interest. The content of the item and material found in the stack of documents provide a glimpse into the strange, frightening and at the same time exhilarating events that have become the main act and have taken a center place on the world stage.

While the information provides a summary of sorts, the story itself is much larger and more complex than could be included in brief correspondence. The tale that flows from the letter is told in as complete and unabridged a version as possible; given the constraints of time and the dictates of parsimony:

> It's Monday
> Dear Dad,
> I assume you are home already. I left this next to the coffee maker knowing you would find it there. I want to give you some of my most guarded thoughts. First, thank you for joining us on the drive to Phoenix. I regret that neither Sherry nor I was pleasant to be around the past few days. I, for one, was so conflicted about leaving everyone that the words were not there. I am so sorry that we couldn't tell you ahead of time. As you know, when Christian called last evening, we were given very little warning before we had to finish packing. I told you earlier we were to be ready. I guess this qualifies as a "moment's notice". I am so glad that you and I discussed this possibility a few days ago. I am happy that we had a chance to prepare the kids as we did last week. I guess there is no real way to thoroughly deal with the emotions felt in things such as this in advance.
> You are appreciated more than you will ever know. You are a hero and my greatest hope as a grandparent; you and Mom together. To be blunt, you have been better parents to my kids than I. Rest assured if I saw any other way to do these things I would pursue it. I don't have to remind you about the damage that people like Rollands can do.

This mission may well be the most important ever. Frankly, that is why Sherry was upset last night. Sherry did not want to leave you, Mom and the kids. It's such an important time in their lives. Since college is in the offing for Katy and Sam is growing up so fast! I wish there was an alternative.

I have told you very little about our task or our challenges and that I regret. You know as much about the project as I can share without putting you and the family in danger. However, I have enclosed a small black and white reproduction of a painting that hangs in the Philadelphia Museum of Art. It is titled Saint Francis Defeats the Antichrist.. It, I am confident, can give you in a visual of the complexities of our challenge and the dangers we face. While this painting was composed hundreds of years ago, many of the problems we confront are the same today. This oil on canvas, in a vivid and shocking way, summarizes our task. Well, it isn't in a physical sense to kill the antichrist, but our mission is simple yet daunting— to stop a mad man before he can sow any more seeds of degeneration.

Pay particular attention to Elijah and his Flaming Sword. Note also, the foot of one of those angelic beings in the upper section of the painting. You will notice what appears to be a cuff around the ankle on one of them. This cuff and the sword are somehow related to our work. At least, that is what I have learned from Sherry. We will know more of the details when we meet with Christian later today in DC. While the topic of the painting can cause repulsion, the beauty and complexity of this art defies description. As usual we are not confronted with beauty. I fear much of this task could be ugly; at least that's what Sherry said.

The copy of the work cannot do the original justice. In a strange way, we will be characters of this painting ourselves, if what I have heard is close to the truth. As you now can attest, she is right more often than not. I want you to be certain that I love you very much and so does Sherry. Please keep reminding the kids that we have left, not because we wanted to, or because of the thrill. To be direct, it is our duty. There is real evil on the earth. That is what we must confront. If we are successful, who knows what wonderful things might happen? Remember if I do not communicate with you for more than a week please contact the youth hostels travel site @www.sanfransisco.org. I trust them as I do those who protect my most guarded secrets.

Love you both, take care!
Jake

1

A STRANGE BEGINNING

Two women were seated next to each other in the first class section of a Boeing 767 aircraft. The seats were purchased for them by the conference planners of the New York Newspaper Writers' Conference. Ann L. Luste joined the flight after a visit to her sister in Renton, Washington. Both she and Ruth Thaif had been selected to attend because they had written award winning series.

Ruth had written about the Cedarvale High School extortion attempt. She was also the reporter that covered the trial and other aspects of the botched heist. She was the first to link Ieke Rollands, a former school superintendent and military general, to the plot. These pieces documented the actors and actions surrounding the abduction of Sherry Paul also known as "Sally Scantz." Ruth had been invited to share her background material on "Sally's" mysterious cave rescue and her long recovery.

Ruth was suffering from a lack of sleep and as such was looking forward to a nice long nap on the plane. On this particular day, a snooze, as it turned out, would be an elusive goal.

Ann was overflowing the space and more than ample in normal chit chat. Ruth knew of and respected Ann's work.

Ann planned to share at the conference, what the Sands newspaper had found and written in the "Chereb fog series." This, in addition to other topics also covered a tragic helicopter crash in Oak Creek Canyon.

Prior to the flight Ruth knew little of Ann's recent works. She was, however, impressed with Ann's status. Nevertheless she was growing weary of the conversation. Her problem was not just Ann.

She was tired of a flight that had not even begun. The pilot had announced delays three times in an hour. Each was caused by low-hanging fog. This strange mist seemed to add light and beauty to what was a typical dreary Seattle SeaTac morning. This appeared to be very same type of meteorological substance of which Ann had written.

Even though it glowed as though it was lighted from the inside, the substance was very dense and it reduced visibility around the terminal. This made take-off and landing almost impossible. The misty-vale was similar to the clouds that were becoming ever more common throughout the world. As it happened, these molecular formations were a major focus of Ann's award winning series.

Her work suggested the golden haze was related to Ieke Rollands and a secret society of underground agents. Scientists, reporters and others had actually criticized Ann's work because she had never explained just how humans could create such events. Just as the plane made its way to the runway and took off, Ruth made the unfortunate or, fortunate step of bringing that fact to Ann's attention.

For Ruth the conversation was about to take a sharp turn. For Ann was not the type to let any simple comment go without a vigorous defense. This weather anomaly in Seattle spawned an opportunity for Ann to expound upon her newspaper reports. But more importantly, she loved to tell stories—especially those others had developed and wrote.

Ann simply said, "I assume you are well aware that it is believed these changes in the weather have been traced to western Spain, Ieke Rollands and Jake Rader. "

"Come on, you can't really believe that there is something mystical associated with the phenomenon?" Ruth asked, attempting to hide her incredulity.

"Well," Ann said, "I do and that requires a response that could take considerable time. You know I am the expert on these matters."

Hoping to catch Ann in her exaggeration Ruth asked, "Hey, we have nothing but time on our hands, right?"

"Okay, but understand that in my opinion, these things have less to do with normal weather and more to do with some kind of warfare; at least, that is what I have been told." Ann replied.

"Who told you that?" Ruth asked.

"Well you know, there are a number of reports of a strange battle. This battle was on the streets of Galicia, Spain. "How come I have read nothing of this war on the wire?" Ruth asked.

"Research scientists and State Department officials are still working on the project and I have directed our staff to interview many of them." Ann responded.

"So really your paper is just speculating at this time right? But go ahead, I am in step," Ruth said.

"You must know of Jake Rader and his wife Sherry, right?" Ann queried.

"Do I know them? Remember, I was the one that broke the story of the whole Ceadervale caper and how Jake left his work to follow Sherry." Ruth said.

"Well let's start right there then. Remember her background?" Ann asked.

"Yes, but what does teaching school have to do with these strange mist events?" Ruth wondered out loud.

"You must know she was not really a teacher." Ann said.

Ann was sure that in order to tell Ruth what she knew and how, indeed the whole extraordinary thing was related to weather she would have to start with a garage in Sedona, Arizona. That is because Clay Berry, a cub reporter for The Sands News, was the one who obtained access to the garage.

As it happened, Clay helped Jake's daughter Katy, after she sustained broken bones and other severe injuries. She was the only surviving victim of a deadly helicopter crash in Oak Creek Canyon. The beautiful valley, just east of Sedona, Arizona had claimed more than its share of lives from accidents-- not to mention suicides and other assorted catastrophes. Many of the locals thought these unfortunate disasters were related to the vortex patterns for which Sedona is famous.

In the days and weeks following, Katy's recovery and recuperation she provided Clay with the key elements used in his reports. Barring that chance encounter none of the information would have been available to the public.

Ann did not think it necessary to provide Ruth all the details of the relationship between Clay and Katy; at least for the moment. Besides, she reasoned, the status of chief editor gave her credentials to communicate certain filtered information. As it turned out she was the main filter anyway.

Ann said, "On the top of a stack of papers nearly three feet high, in a place owned by Jake was a note. The hand-written material had no date. One might assume that it was one of the latest written, given its place at the top of the others. It merely said, 'We have found what we are after and now we are on our way home. Please keep this box of articles and notes. I will go through them when I return home. Jake'"

As she finished the sentence the plane in which they were traveling passed through one the strange fog banks and lurched to the side. The passengers almost in unison let out a gasp. It was almost like Ann had queued up the event for dramatic emphasis. As this golden fog filled the cabin, the tension and anxiety hung on like leaches.

Ann looked over at Ruth who was white as a hardboiled egg and as still as a praying mantis. Ann smiled in a way that helped Ruth begin to relax.

Sensing that the scare was over Ann began tell Ruth where the pieces of the story came from.

"The hand-written piece contained a small sketch of a church. While it was difficult to know the exact whereabouts of the Chapel, the paper on which it was sketched provided a clue. The note was written on paper from a Hotel Paradores, in Galicia, Spain. It must have been composed by Jake because it was signed, we assume, by him.

"Remember that it was in this pile of articles and letters from around the world. In addition, fastened with a paper clip, were stories cut out of newspapers from South America. The central theme of the material, as we discovered, was the sordid practice of grave robbing."

"Grave robbing! Not like stealing the deformed skills found in Peru." Ruth interjected.

"Yes and distributed throughout the items were other hand-done pieces, many related to St. Francis of Assisi. You know the main church in Galicia, Spain is his namesake. But that's not all.

"Along with the note, on the top of the stack was a printed copy of the painting titled, St. Francis Defeats the Antichrist.

On the white border of the picture, in black ink, is the name Ieke Rollands with an arrow pointing to the antichrist. This antichrist is the central person in the composition. The piece of work is shockingly eerie."

"The whole topic freaks me out; I get a creepy feeling with the religious stuff," Ruth added.

"Well then this will blow your mind. A number of personal letters were distributed throughout the papers as well. Many of these pieces seemed to refer to actual events depicted in the painting. We found that a simple substitution of 'Sherry and Jake' for St. Francis, helped us piece the story together," Ann explained in a pedantic tone.

"Didn't Saint Francis live in the thirteenth century? I heard that he wasn't even a priest. I know he had and has a broad and deep impact on life throughout the world," Ruth managed to suggest.

"You must know that his sainthood was not given out of a longstanding family Catholic Church connection. That's why Jake was quite taken with him." Ann continued.

"That makes sense. People told us that Jake was fascinated by religious history," Ruth replied.

Ann continued, "Jake, you know, had only been in the Sedona house a short time. He must have been quite a writer too. He authored many of the personal notes and letters and he may well have drawn the arrow on the side of the black and white reproduction. At least that is what the handwriting suggested. Most of the documentation seemed to have been collected by Jake's father."

"Okay I have it. Jake is my Jake right? You know the Jake that I reported leaving his job as principal and marrying Sally, I mean Sherry. Correct?" Ruth clarified.

"Right, according to Jake's daughter Katy, Jake and his wife Sherry were fascinated by the painting. That could be why the picture was found near the top of the stack." Ann said.

"So what else did you discover there?" Ruth Asked.

"In this small upscale community, people wondered why Jake and Sherry would leave family and friends to go on a 'wild harebrained adventure.'" Ann Said.

"Yes! That is what people were saying about Jake. They saw his leaving in the middle of the year when he was a principal in Seattle as quite irresponsible. I see it differently don't you?" Ruth asked.

"Well, the materials uncovered in the stack of papers provided many clues that led to a theory as to why they felt they had to leave. Yet the records did not answer all the questions." Ann Said.

"You mean they gave you a little peek into their world." Ruth suggested.

"Yes and did you know that Sedona, Arizona is just a few hours north of Phoenix?" Ann asked.

"Come on, how does this have anything to do with the crazy weather and your warfare claim?" Ruth asked.

"Trust me, it does, but you will have to be patient. I can tell you that sifting through all the papers was just the beginning. These and a journal, plus personal accounts, were organized and originally shared publically by the Phoenix Sands Newspaper and ya know, I edited most of them. This information, a number of exclusives by Clay Berry is the background for the saga." Ann said.

"Well I know Jake kept copious notes. I learned that while I was doing the story on Jake in Seattle," Ruth asserted.

"Anyway, the journal entries and the other materials gave Clay all the background for the theme that spanned many continents and centuries of history. But that's not all; access to the key elements of the ancient material was approved by a caretaker on a small island, on a lake, in the middle of Italy. I can't give you his name because he wants to remain anonymous. I can tell you this; the whole thing is, as you might guess, strange and creepy." Ann said.

"I do remember Kareem Razier, a former partner of Ieke Rollands. He and Ieke went missing sometime back without a trace, as did Jake and his wife Sherry. But I didn't know about the island." Ruth filled in.

"You were totally unaware?" Ann insisted with a quizzical smile. "So you haven't read any of Clay's stories in the Sands?"

"Truthfully, I do remember a snippet or two. You know, we followed Ieke Rollands and his exploits in Seattle." Ruth Said.

"So, anyway I admit, was it not for the nice work of Clay, a very young inexperienced writer you know, who writes for me, this reconstruction of the events could not have been possible. In addition to gaining access to the garage items, Clay discovered that Razier is living as a kind of mystic philosopher in the hills not far from Assisi, Italy. I believe he thinks Jake and Sherry are either in South America or are missing and assumed dead. I don't think anyone knows."

"Yeah, that is so weird and so sad. I feel so sorry for Jake's daughter Katy." Ruth said.

2

BEGINNING THE END

Ieke was after his prize. This was the third day in a row that he was digging in a valley not far from Cusco, Peru. The Urubamba River region of that country is known for many ancient cultural artifacts. He had not discovered another room or burial area. He was angry.

He marched to the top of a large pile of dirt and rocks; wearing the medallion of The Knights of St. John. He kicked the ground spreading gravel and sand in all directions.

"It is because of me that you all have a chance for a better life. You have let me down in so many ways and I will not take your laziness and lack of loyalty any longer. You know it is I and I alone whom you must follow without question, understand? He thundered."

"Keep moving you slugs," Kareem Razier, Ieke's right hand man yelled.

A gnome like fellow at the end of the line translated "Mas rapido Burros!"

"Have you found any more?" Ieke quizzed.

A young man with dark eyes, jet black hair, and a large sun darkened nose replied, "No mas, Jeffe!"

Hearing that, Ieke's face turned bright red, his jaw stiffened and he ripped his shirt open. Cream colored buttons flew across the ground. He launched himself over the edge of the pile of rubble and grabbed the young man on both sides of the chest. He lifted him off the ground nearly two feet and slammed him down onto the rocky, sandy soil.

Ieke Rollands ranted. "I don't need talk from you! I need action! What do you think I'm paying you for, you worthless pigs?"

The picks and shovels landed more frequently as the pace of digging quickened. Farther down the tunnel, below the group, Kareem Razier, Ieke's loyal assistant, trudged slowly up the Hill. At the same time, the totally humiliated young Peruvian worker slid back into the hole and began throwing dirt out of the tunnel using his broken handled shovel.

Razier walked up to Ieke and said in a low almost inaudible voice, "If you want them to help you, don't push so hard. I know we haven't found any more pots or anything to sell, but it's not their fault."

Ieke turned his face slowly to Razier and snarled, "Stay out of this; you just make sure these donkeys keep at it."

With that, Razier fixed his black eyes on Ieke for nearly twenty seconds. Slowly, very slowly, he turned and walked back down the steep terrain.

Ieke laughed with a touch of sarcasm and mumbled, "Do you think these grunts deserve your respect, you sniveling Jack-ass?"

The plunder Ieke was after however, was something even more fantastic. He was after the Clavicularius pars Cephas. This pair of items was a subject of discussion and debate for thousands of years. Ieke was convinced that the Keys, as they were sometimes called, were in this vicinity. He reached into his pocket and pulled out the piece of the map he stole from the Old Man's papers earlier.

The Old Man was a mentor and friend to the knights. He was known for his wisdom, fairness and just actions. Now older and more withered, the Old Man was still highly revered by most knights. Rollands, however had taken advantage of the Old Man for his self-interests often. If he was able to find what he was after, he would be halfway to unimaginable power and fame. More than the money, that's what drove Ieke Rollands.

3

GROSS AND EXPLOITIVE

The flight attendant walked down the aisle, offering snacks. Ann grabbed a package of peanuts barely pausing to take a breath. Most of the other passengers paid little attention as she continued on through the coach cabin.

"You haven't heard the half of it." Ann said, "Many are quite concerned and, in some cases, panicked over the changes in weather and atmospheric conditions."

"Aren't you?" Ruth added.

Ann leaned in close to Ruth, touching her shoulder. She whispered, "I hope you will take this in the proper light. Have you heard what people in Sedona are saying about the weather? It is strongly believed that the cosmological events and the strange auras have intensified in Sedona and are now somewhat regular and seem to be spreading. I am almost sure the crash was related."

"That's what I told you earlier. We saw the sparkles on the runway in Seattle; they are beautiful and weird all at the same time. They almost look alive. But it has only happened like two or three times there." Ruth said.

"Anyway," Ann said, "it is believed by most of us that these events are somehow connected."

"What events?" Ruth asked.

"Clay and others have suggested that there is a link to Jake and Sherry; and in a strange way, to Galicia, Spain." Ann said.

"How can that be?" Ruth asked.

"You remember that Ieke Rollands was a retired army general?" Ann quizzed.

"Sure I do." Ruth said.

"Well, he, not very long ago, was seen in Spain. But nobody knows what happened to him. Last I heard he was down in Peru. Didn't you write that he had gone to South America when authorities tried to track him down? Turns out he was digging for artifacts and such. He still was a Knight of Saint John but he was ransacking the area and raping the land." Ann explained.

"He was a cocky and arrogant one, wasn't he?" Ruth asked.

"As I live and breathe, anyway…"

Ruth interrupted, "I understand the knights were a group of people who, while always there, moved in the shadows working for good? So I don't quite get how he could be the guy you are describing."

"The purpose of the knights, we found, is to shed light on truth and to stand on the side of good where evil exists. At least that is what many of the written documents indicated. Mind you, it was hard to find much reliable information. The Sands reported previously on the speculations and hypotheses concerning the background of the group. It's without serious debate that the group is still active.

"Ieke Rollands, according to this guy Christian, was still a knight when he tore up the graves. He then sold the contents.

Collectors and traders from around the world were paying good money for native textiles or old cotton and woolen items. I, like you, don't quite get him either." Ann said.

Ruth interjected, "I understand human remains from the pre-Inca period are even more prized, if they demonstrate evidence of the strange practice of body-parts manipulation undertaken in the area for centuries."

"Yes in a perverted, sensual kind of way." Ann continued.

"Have you seen the large skulls that some people think are alien? Ruth asked.

"Well yes but only in books." Ann said.

4

BRUTAL INSANE HUMANITY

Mr. Goodman kissed his wife of six years and pecked his little son on the head as he patted his hairless, skinny dog. He made his way out of his small shack. He coughed deeply as he moved to the dusty street not far from Cusco Peru. He suffered from the years of damage done to his lungs by the dust and mold contained in the mines and caves in which he had worked since he was a mere boy. The Sacred Valley of the Inca, as it was called, served as a rich source of agriculture, mining and culture for thousands of years.

For Goodman, it was merely a place to survive. While he was in his early thirties, he strode with the gait of an old man. As he stepped onto the dusty road, a large white van slid to a stop. He joined friends and fellow workers inside. The large plumes of dust followed the rig as it wound its way up the rough road following the Urubamba River to the northwest.

People in his village said, "He is such a good man!" Of course that is the English translation. Goodman took his name as an honor to the owner of the last mine he helped to exploit. He, like many of the recruits, knew how to dig and that is what he did. Yet his was not just a minor role; he was a respected community member.

The auto stopped after a short trip down a short path, off the main road. It was approximately 7:30 AM as Goodman and another ten Peruvian laborers made their way down the long dark tunnel connecting the ram-shackled house to the new digs; not more than fifty yards from the small chapel.

The church was dedicated to Saint Peter and it bears his name. Clearly visible on the left front façade is a large figure of the Saint holding two Keys in crossed arms. The chapel covers the ruins of an ancient Incan palace dedicated to the sun god. People visiting the chapel had no idea what was going on just below their feet.

Goodman led the small group toward the miniature hut that hid the entrance to the tunnel where they dug. Ieke was already inside working his way to the newly discovered room.

"It has got to be here," Rollands said as he slid down the last few feet. "I hate this desolate and foreboding place. The main altar of the Incan temple of the sun is just above me. Look at these stones. See how seamlessly they fit together. This is not Spanish work; this is Inca. This room has got to be it. It is here I feel it."

Razier and Rollands had arrived a few minutes ahead of the laborers. The rest of the group paid little attention to Ieke's ramblings as they filtered in.

Outside, as usual, the sun was beating down on the old sod brick structure even at this early vestige of morning. The hut served as the entry chamber to the underground hall that led to the rooms. The Peruvian workers packed pics and shovels over their shoulders and chanted as it was their practice each day.

Razier joked as they slid along, "Hi he hi ditty ho ho, I feel like the woodsman in Snow-white and the seven dwarfs."

Ieke did not respond. The dig site itself was approximately ten meters wide by twenty meters long; nearly a quarter the size of a football field.

While none of it was exposed to the heat of the sun, much of the area was covered over by centuries of sand and rock. Much of the small ancient dwelling was still intact, small rooms protruding from the large open area. Not more than 40 km down the road was the large and somewhat restored ruins of Ollantaytambo.

It was the wayside palace that was used by the Inca on travels from Cusco to Machu Picchu, Peru. The site was also not far from the modern and prosperous Cusco, to the west, over the hills. Goodman called this place home. The sacred valley is dotted with small villages and claims a long history of conquest that did not begin with the Spaniards and would not end with Ieke Rollands.

Ieke sat down on the dirt and rock floor next to a stone vent in the area open to the rays of the sun. The light now traced its way down the shaft providing the only natural illumination. Razier knew Ieke was becoming agitated because he was mumbling and reading. He was intently reviewing the records contained in the journal of Alonzo De Alvarado. Alonzo De Alvarado was the knight of the order of Santiago who was charged with the defense of Cusco in the early 1500s.

According to Alvarado, he paused in this very spot on a sunny hill not far off the road, one day's ride south east of Cusco. Alonso De Alvarado was the nephew of Pedro De Alvarado. Pedro was the conquistador who became Governor of Guatemala. Ieke had stolen the journal a few weeks earlier from the catacombs under St. François's Monastery which was in Lima. He and Razier dug through the nearly ten feet of femur bones that hid the journal for centuries.

Razier remembered spending an entire night replacing the bones into the intricate serape pattern that they formed. Rollands used the archives of the knights and material he stole from the Old Man to find this important historical document.

"Remember when we dug through the bones under Saint Francis's Monastery? I reminded you that the femurs were laid in the same exact pattern as the Keys over the door of the Basilica in the main square, Ieke. Maybe we need to move under the main doors of the church." Kareem said.

Ieke said, "I'm sure this is the place."

"Maybe there was another Temple in the area." Razier reminded him.

"No this has to be it." Ieke said.

While they had taken a small golden shield, some pottery and two large skulls from the dig, they did not find what Ieke wanted.

"Alvarado had the Chereb and Clavicularius right here." He mumbled.

He felt he had reason to be frustrated and as a result could be edgy because his funds were running low and he was worried that he might be discovered. The vendors he hired to sell various artifacts taken from other sites were demanding more money because of the increasing risks they were taking.

It didn't help that Kareem Raizer constantly reminded Ieke that they were in danger of discovery. While he had been paying off highly placed officials, they too were asking for a bigger share of his dwindling profits. But his most pressing problem was that all this was really a cover for his ultimate objective—the Clavicularius and the Chereb.

Over the years there was speculation and frank conversation between Christian Poincy and other Knights of St. John, Ieke Rollands included, that at least one of the Keys resided in Peru. While Alvarado's death and burial documents contain conflicting information, there was evidence that special powers were given to Alonzo De Alvarado by Queen Isabella herself centuries before.

Most knights knew that the St. Johns were aligned with the Knights of Santiago. Alonzo De Alvarado was a member of the Santiago's and his orders came straight from the crown. The Queen planned to move the sacred items from safely-hidden spots in Europe to the New World. In fact, the historical records show that in 1534 Alvarado went to fight with his Uncle and Francisco Pizarro not to find gold but as some knights believed, to bury gold and to hide the source of his power. Knowing that Alvarado failed in his mission and Alvarado was buried somewhere close to where Rollands was digging was the very thing that was making Ieke Rollands a crazy man.

Kareem Razier who did much of Rollands' bidding was becoming suspicious. Razier was learning that Ieke was not doing the work of God as Ieke said, but was doing just the opposite.

Kareem emerged from the tunnel, walked over to Rollands and said, "I fear you're pushing these kids too hard and they are beginning to mumble."

Rollands looked up slowly from the document and said, "There are many bodies in these valleys. The hills don't care whether you are a native, Muslim, Jew, Christian or heathen; they accept the dead no matter what the persuasion."

With that, Razier turned and walked slowly back to the small piles of rocks that were beginning to appear on the far side of the sandy, rocky ruins. The laborers continued to dig and to chant. This too bothered Rollands-- for he did not know what they were singing.

Not more than two minutes later Rollands got up from his perch. He walked over to where one of the smallest men was standing. He was knee-deep in a small bowl that his pick and shovel created. Rollands grabbed the shovel from the young Peruvian. Swinging it like a golf club he made contact with the young man's head. A loud thud was heard—like the sound of a melon falling of the end of a delivery truck. The victim fell to his knees and slumped into the hole.

Rollands drew the shovel back at least four times and continued to bring it down on to the now shattered head of Goodman. Razier felt medium velocity blood hit on his arm. He recoiled and moved away. The nose and one ear of Goodman's face were mostly gone. The bright red and blue mass of bone fragments and blood that was a head minutes earlier; was now a grotesque platter of plasma. The splatter even hit Razier in the face.

Looking directly at Razier, Rollands began to shovel dirt over the twitching and yet lifeless body. He threw the shovel into the hole and walked away. As Rollands turned away Razier slipped a small note on the far side of the freshly formed grave.

"Now let that be a lesson to all of you. If you expect to be on this crew, then I don't want to find out that there was talk about our work or any more slackish effort out of anyone. In his case he talked too much and worked too little. Get back to your holes and dig." Rollands yelled through gritted teeth.

Blood mixed with sweat rolled down his face and onto his shirt as he moved back and forth from one side of the cave to the other— looking and acting like a caged lion.

Kareem Razier now saw Rollands as so many others had seen him. Rollands was driven by a quest for power and wealth; the kind of man that would do whatever might be necessary to satisfy his twisted desires. It was said that Alvarado, over time, suffered from the same disease that Rollands did; an unhealthy belief in himself as the source of his talent and success. In the end Alvarado died alone, devastated and without peace.

Razier wondered to himself. *Why was I so blind for so long. He is not doing this for Allah. In his view everyone exists to accomplish his own goals. He is evil.* Kareem Raizer decided to bide his time, but he would not be Rolland's errand boy much longer.

For now and for obvious reasons Rollands decided it was time to move on.

5

THE BROKEN NEST

The plane flew through choppy air as the fasten seat belt sign was illuminated. Ann pulled the cinch a bit tighter as she cleared her throat. She rubbed her eyes as turned back to Ruth. Before she could continue Ruth interrupted.

Speaking like an excited teen-ager, Ruth said, "So you are saying that Rollands was a jerk just as we in Seattle thought—remind me who Christian was?"

"In a minute, in a minute," Ann said.

"You remember Rollands' physique?" Ann asked with a twinkle in her eye.

"He had to be in his late 50's. I imagine Ieke was still a hunk, with muscles hanging out all over. I know he had stamina; he probably could run younger military officers to exhaustion?" Ruth suggested.

"Don't doubt it for an instant," Ann said. "So, the wind was blowing and he was breathing deep and with great force as he barked out orders for the randomly-recruited ruffians."

Ann laughed out loud, and then she regained her normal stoic composure. She bent her head forward and peered over the top of her large, black rimmed glasses hopping nobody had heard her outburst.

"This group was composed of small mostly adolescent-appearing native men who were digging in clay-filled soil laced with rocks. They used wood-handled picks and shovels. They were working in a valley southeast, and about thirty or forty kilometers from Cusco, Peru.

"They worked underground below a clay and mud-bricked hut, near the church of St. Peter, in Andahuaylillas. They were digging out an old tunnel just east of the footings of an Incan temple, dedicated to the Sun. The temple sat under and provided the foundation for the church in the town square." Ann said.

Ann went on, "Rollands was energized because he had just made a large sale to a private collector who paid a huge sum, close to one million Nuevo Sols, for a rare and unique blanket from the pre-Incan early intermediate period. It was represented to be Moche. This was found in a burial mound just outside Cusco. It was a fine profit on the black market."

"Now that's information. Where did you get that?" Ruth asked.

"Let's say there are many who don't like crazy American generals messing up their history." Ann Said.

"Yeah," Ruth said, "the Incan civilization was built on much older cultures as you say, Moche was one but there were many others like the Nazca and Pucara."

"So you can see why Rollands was not on the best of terms with the knights." Ann said.

"Okay, but let's back up. I don't follow what was the big deal about the artwork in the garage. Where did Jake get the painting and why were he and Sherry so taken with it?" Ruth inquired as she readjusted her seat belt. "Enough of this this relationship stuff, didn't you say that he was sent maps of Italy and other parts of the world?"

Ann said, "He was also studying Italy, but he was troubled and conflicted. He struggled to find the links both to the painting and how it apprehends the present and the past." Ann said.

"Well what do Italy and Guatemala have in common for our purposes?" Ruth asked.

"He also wrestled with the demons he would have to face and those he would confront shortly. I really think he was using the painting as some sort of road map or something, don't you?" Ann asked looking up at the ceiling.

"So tell me more about where they lived in Sedona. I really want to get a feel for what they gave up." Ruth directed.

"Well, the home that Jake and Sherry purchased was sufficient—," Ann said.

"What do you mean sufficient?" Ruth interrupted.

"Quite small but adequate," Ann continued

"That's right Jake had two kids," Ruth said.

Ann said, "Don't forget Jake's parents. The kids were older now, they needed their own rooms."

Ann continued, "The three-bedroom, three bathroom place was newer, with an exterior of stucco and finished in a way that celebrated Spanish details and modern appliances. The home also was fitted with a two-car garage.

"Did Jake and Sherry still drive Jake's 1993 rosewood-colored Honda Accord? It was a junker wasn't it?" Ruth asked.

"There were plans for a newer nicer car, 'when they could afford one'. In 'The Village', everything was accessible by foot; at least all the important things. Jakes parents walked to restaurants and small shops, even the grocery stores. His kids walked to a private school provided by the knights. However a second car would be in everyone's interest." Ann said

"Okay, so that is where they hung out and prepared; so what else did you discover?" Ruth asked. She was now wide-a-wake and interested.

"Anyway, Katy told Clay, something like her dad spent more time and energy learning about the fifth crusade, than he did with the kids, that's why they would often try to get him side-tracked. But that all ended abruptly. On one particular day Sherry returned from a six mile run to the top of Bell Rock and back." Ann said.

Weren't we discussing the house size?" Ruth Asked.

"So I doubt the house size really mattered. They were outside a lot!" Ann said.

"I imagine she was in really good shape," Ruth said.

"Trust me; this running up Bell Rock was a feat that any athlete would see as a great challenge. One must consider this extraordinary, especially with the injuries she endured during imprisonment. She weighed nearly 125 pounds, a gain of close to half the weight she was after she was released from the cave not that many months earlier." Ann said.

"Wow, according to the hospital records in Seattle, she was lucky to be alive, let alone in that kind of shape." Ruth said.

I think Sherry knew more than she told Jake. According to Jake's mother, Sherry was clear about how she must withdraw from not only the kids but also Jake's mother and Jake's dad. Somehow Jake's mother sensed that Sherry was preparing for more than just another project." Ann said.

"Why do you say that she didn't give Jake the whole story?" Ruth Asked.

Jake wrote about it in his journal. It said 'Sherry, My bride, I love you. I can't believe it's been over a year––.'" Ann said.

"Wow you like this don't you," Ruth asked.

Ann continued, "The journal also gave us insight into Sherry and her condition and I quote, 'She moved slowly, almost haltingly, in my direction.' He also noted her limping after the run, He could tell she had aggravated the old injury; but today something more painful slowed her gate I think. She carried a dreaded gold colored, envelope. These small gold envelopes, Jake wrote, 'mean one thing. She knew it and I knew it.'"

"Weather, we were talking about weather, remember?" Ruth asked hoping to redirect the conversation.

"I need to say a bit more. The moment she entered the room Jake sensed her presence as she moved in his direction. Jake looking up from the material immediately recognized the gold paper as what they feared. It was a simple note from Christian Poincy. This was not the first of such things he and Sherry had received from Christian. Christian is the Sigma Knight who is responsible for the entire United States operation." Ann said.

"Hey wait a minute," Ruth demanded. "Is this for real or are you spinning a yarn for me?"

Ann looked over, squinted her puffy eyes and said, "You better believe it; I could not make this stuff up. Christian was the source of many communications but the gold note was different."

"So I assume Christian was a mentor and guide for Jake and Sherry, as they, like ghosts, fought against those who aimed to diminish the American life. You know truth, justice en' all that!" Ruth said.

Ann said, "Well, as an east coast attorney with ample connections he guided first, Sherry, and later Jake, with background, education and mentoring. Yet it goes beyond that.

He was a friend to and a cheerleader for both of them. It was nearly a year since Jake or Sherry heard personally from him. It seemed like just days before Jake and Sherry were married and spent a wonderful week on a honeymoon in Austria at Christian's expense."

"Got it, but I don't need to know about the wedding. I already wrote about all that. So what was in the gold envelope?" Ruth asked.

"She timidly moved over to Jake with a hint of a tear in her eye. Jake barely took note of Sherry as he focused on the gold paper. She didn't have to say anything. Jake knew what was in the envelope. It was new orders and he knew that their time in their protected hideaway was short. It was a nice year with new identities and new beginnings." Ann said.

"So they were only back with the kids a year or so," Ruth suggested.

Ann said, "They lived like a real family. Now that was all about to end. Jake dreaded this day. On the other hand he knew about duty and obligation and frankly excitement ahead. As Sherry handed him the envelope he felt the strength leave his hand. He could barely wrap his fingers around the paper as he began to open the package. Jake pulled the page from the container. All it said was:

> **Hello Jake,**
> **I hope all finds you and Sherry well and in good spirits. I will call this evening."**
>
> **CDP'"**

"That was it! Are you kidding me!" Ruth exclaimed.

6

REALITY SETS IN

Late in the evening when they thought everyone except he and Sherry were in bed, the phone rang. Jake picked it up and walked to the courtyard. Sherry followed.

Jake flipped it open and hit the speaker button and said, 'hello."

"It's Christian, the voice on the other end said. "Jake we have exciting news for you. After nearly a year of searching we have discovered our rogue Ieke is living in Peru. At least we have solid evidence pointing in that direction."

"So we are confident he still is in South America." Sherry whispered.

"How did you find him?" Jake asked.

"Agents intercepted what we have confirmed as correspondence between Ieke and Carlos. You remember Carlos; he's the guy we put away in Seattle and was still serving out his sentence for conspiracy to commit theft of government property amongst other things. He will be handed over to Spanish authorities shortly to answer for a murder in Spain.

"Anyway, I guess I should get to the point. I am asking you and Sherry to track Ieke down and to neutralize any plans he may now have. From what we know, Ieke has made a big discovery. I don't need to bog you down with the details except to say this, no doubt, is your most dangerous assignment yet." Christian said.

Sherry hurried back into the house as Jake closed off the conversation with Christian. A few minutes later Jake found Sherry sitting under the stars with her head down in the front courtyard.

He said, "Christian gave us the details and specific instructions. He also said we are to pick up final orders and material that we need for the trip from his office." Jake looked at Sherry with misty eyes.

Jake slowly sat down on the small table beside her. He looked up at Sherry through tears and started, "Well my love, you and I both knew we couldn't hide in our little mountain nest forever."

He reached out his arms and captured Sherry in his grasp. They held each other until the blood drained from their arms.

What they didn't know was that Katy was watching and listening from her bedroom window.

"What will you tell your folks and the kids?" Sherry asked slowly.

For a few moments Jake considered the deep implications contained in her simple question.

"Like you I am more than a little concerned that we might permanently damage the family. Let's take a walk under the stars." Jake said slowly through clinched teeth.

As they walked out of the garden Katy heard, "I know what we have to do. You and I can work out a plan to tell everyone. Are you all right with that Sherry?"

Katy shed a tear as she sat and listened.

During the two hour drive to Phoenix, Jake blocked out the pain of his decision with the details of the task before them.

Jake was focused the day before; he spent time studying materials sent to him by Christian, the brief history of the conquistadores of Central and South America. He understood both the benefits and the downside associated with the Spanish civilization in the Americas. He remembered analyzing a copy of a major piece of art work that at one time hung in the convent of Saint Francis and the Knights of Saint James in the old capital city of Guatemala, Antigua. The reality of his decision was now behind him. He was committed. There was no turning back.

I need to know more; why is there Jewish, Christian and Muslim iconography in it. I wonder if the work was designed to make a political statement. Was this masterpiece propaganda and as such why would Christian send it as part of his preparation?"

When Jake posed that very question to Sherry on their walk the night before, she mentioned, "It provides truth, even for today."

What is this truth Sherry was referring to?

Jake asked himself, "Why was this important for people in the 17th century? Specifically, what was the point to be made to the nuns and religious students of the convent? They relied on two dimensional arts as an important source of facts. Did they see what we see on both sides of the battle? With no internet or chat rooms to add information could they really grasp the depth of the work? Was the paint on this 65" by 60"canvas laid down by this skilled master divinely inspired, the work of a devil or just blind luck?"

The painting now rests in Philadelphia Pennsylvania. That was yesterday. Today his task is committing to memory all of the larger lakes in central Italy. No matter how much he tries to get his work done, his thoughts go back to the artwork. He could not get the painting out of his head.

Jake turned slowly as he put his shoes and belt in the plastic container at the Phoenix airport. He was thinking about the note he had written to his dad. He was grief-stricken. He could not speak about the emotions that he felt having to leave the family again; even to Sherry. He hoped the letter he had written would be taken in the right spirit. His eyes surveyed Katy's grief-reddened face.

He did not allow his eyes to make contact with hers. He slowly raised his left hand and smiled at Sam who seemed zombie like. Jake's mom and dad moved their hands in a slow and deliberate fashion. They knew full well they may not see Jake or Sherry again. Sherry was a step ahead of Jake and just entering the magnetic scanner. In a few short hours they would be meeting with Christian. In the meantime, they both in their own way dealt with consequences of their decisions.

They chose to be at Christian's beck and call. Sherry remembered that it was a personal choice to go underground and work for the good, countering the powerful and evil. Even though she had paid dearly she still knew she was doing what was right. Jake already missed the kids.

A 767 sat on the rainbow colored, dew covered tarmac. Nearly 200 passengers slowly made their way to preassigned seats. Two female cabin crew members slowly slid along the entire length of the airplane assisting with overhead luggage. Just after 2:00 PM the head flight attendant spoke on the internal speaker system providing last-minute instructions. At just 15 minutes after the assigned take-off time the plane began to jerk slowly backwards. Jake thought about how awkward and unwieldy the plane was as it slowly rolled away from the terminal. Jake could not help but wonder how long it would be until he saw his family again.

The plane, now under its own power slowly rattled and creaked toward the end of the runway.

Jake turned to Sherry and said, "This is one of the hardest things I've ever had to do."

Sherry smiled and said calmly, "This will be the least of your problems Jake. That is why I felt myself pulling away from Sam, Katy and your parent's weeks ago. This is our lot Jake. For better or worse we are again committed to something greater than ourselves."

The plane was not in the air more than five minutes when Jake began to leaf through the contents of the documents supplied by Christian just a few days earlier. One document was of particular interest to Jake. It described the hideous practice of grave robbing in Peru. Some of the world's largest and oldest treasures had made their way into the private collections of the rich and famous.

This truth had been a right of the wealthy for centuries. Even in the recent excavations at Machu Picchu and in the Cuzco area, as well as the diggings in the Pisco River Delta, grave robbers were decimating archaeological sites and destroying ancient burial grounds.

One article in particular described how thieves tore the tops out of burial sites and stole numerous irreplaceable artifacts. Most recently it was discovered that thieves dug through the catacombs of the burial grounds of the Franciscan

Monastery in Lima. This area contained much evidence of the conflict ridden legacy of Alvarado, Pizarro and the other conquistadors. Jake was pretty sure that Ieke was at the bottom of some of the devastation.

"Would you like something to drink?" The flight attendant asked.

"Yes water and tomato juice please." Sherry said.

Jake shook his head in affirmation, "water please," he said.

The flight touched down at Reagan National at approximately 8:03 PM eastern standard time.

7

WASHINGTON, DC CONFAB

After Jake pulled the last suitcase off the carousel and placed it on the cart, Sherry grabbed him and gave him a big squishy hug. Gradually the hug turned into a mutual embrace; still arm in arm they walked slowly in the direction of the ground transportation area. Sherry had a heavy almost "otherworldly" intensity in her countenance. A car and driver were waiting in the pickup area as assigned. It was just a short drive from Reagan National to Christian's office.

They arrived at approximately 9:15 PM. As Jake and Sherry made their way out of the car, Christian was standing at the entry door of the old brownstone. While he still commanded an image of dignity in his dark blue suit and square shoulders, the years had begun to make their mark. He somehow looked thinner and much grayer to Jake. Sherry moved ahead of Jake. Christian looking tired reached out his arms and pulled Sherry toward him.

"I like you as a blonde," he said.

"It's been a very long time, oh ancient one," Jake said with a smile.

"I'm sure it has not been long enough. I like your beard." Christian said with his half-lipped smile.

He beckoned them into the room. Sherry and Jake had seen it so many times before. Christian's office had a large dark cherry paneled main room with a small on-suite with a shower, toilet and sink. One entire wall approximately, 25 feet long, was filled with log books and various historic titles. As Jake scanned the office, he stopped and took note of one title, "Jefferson's Extracts from the Gospels." He made no comment but later wrote down the reference in his leather-bound journal.

He took in the beauty of the artifacts adorning the room. The large sword in its scabbard was of particular interest. It looked like it was from the Spanish conquest era.

"It's from the early 16th century." Christian said, "Go ahead, check it out."

Jake pulled the blade from the case and looked at the curved, sharpened edge. He wondered what battles it must have seen. Was this a sword used in Peru? Was Christian one of those of whom he had reading?

Jake had been in the office before, but he was still spellbound by the size and quality of the artifacts and the library collection. He was mystified by the fact that he had not seen or at least recalled some of these items. Sherry walked over and sat down on the large leather sofa. After a moment, Jake took a seat next to her.

An assortment of books and documents lined the entire outside edge of the glass and wrought-iron table. What caught Jake's eye was a skin laid out on the middle of the glass. He was particularly intrigued as he noticed the frayed corners of the significantly damaged document. Nearly one third of the length of the right-hand lower quadrant was missing. Sherry focused on the plane and hotel reservations lying at the other end of the table. She noticed her name on the packet cover.

Christian slid his large leather office chair to the opposite side of the desk and sat down.

"I knew you would be tired and hungry, so I ordered a pizza dinner. We can work and eat at the same time, if that's alright?"

"I'm ready to chow down," Jake said, "far as I'm concerned that's fantastic."

"I hope you ordered vegetarian Sherry added. She was grinning as she shot a glance over at Jake.

"It so happens, I ordered one of each," Christian said.

Jake was smiling as he sat there looking at Sherry's knee as if to say, you know what I like.

"Well let's get started," Christian said. "As you know we have finally narrowed Ieke Rollands' location down to a small region of South America. It has taken months to find him but we are now reasonably sure we know where he is. At least we know enough to send a team after him. I know you and Sherry can handle it Jake, but I'm sending the Old Man with you. You understand don't you?"

Jake did not respond he was again focused on the calf-skin document. Somehow he knew it was the key to the day's meeting.

"Sherry you may need to translate for me, especially since much of what I will need to say is in Spanish and Italian." Christian related, "Then we can begin."

Christian picked up the damaged-vellum document from the middle of the table.

"I noticed you have a lot of interest in this Jake."

"That's for sure," Jake said.

"Well it should give you answers to the whole story that I couldn't tell you before." Christian said.

"As you know, when you were in Seattle, there were a lot of strange things that happened. We could not risk that either of you might be compromised. Now, Jake, this particular document is precisely the reason I was not totally square with you."

"Are you talking about Sherry's rescue?" Jake asked.

"Yes I am," Christian said.

"In fact," he continued, "I have here a letter from the Old Man that should clear things up for you."

Christian handed Jake a large envelope. Jake opened the container and began to read:

> Jake,
>
> Sherry knows what I am writing so there is no need for you to read it to her. Feel free to ask her any questions you might have after digesting it. First, I know that you were very upset and confused about the events in Mesa Verde as well as the specific details surrounding Sherry's rescue and subsequent hospitalization in Seattle.
>
> Keep in mind that the life you have chosen, as with life in general, cannot be totally explained by your earthly senses. There are dimensions beyond your experience and outside your current understanding. Sherry can guide you and will be a source of strength.
>
> With that said, I want you to know that you were spot on. Ieke was at the rescue of Sherry in Mesa Verde, in the four corners. You were not dreaming about the fight that you had with him either.

Ieke later flew his plane south out of Seattle. What I did not and could not tell you at the time, was that he was in the process of blackmailing us. At least he attempted to embarrass us regarding the so-called "Cedarvale episode." Let me be clear, Ieke Rollands may think that he has the entire map of some very special artifacts but he does not. That's where you guys come in.

There are three very important relics that have been guarded by the knights over the centuries. Until just recently, Christian had no knowledge of where the third element might be. I tell you that I know where all the items are. One of the two Keys or more accurately described as Cuffs that make up the Clavicularius Pars Cephas was secretly returned to North America after the conquests of the Americas.

Some think that the two Cuffs, as they are called, are in South America. However, we know this is not true. What Ieke does not know is that the document Christian holds clearly shows at least the third artifact, the Chereb, was returned to Europe after the Spanish rule. Sherry knows much more than you realize. Please trust Sherry and all will be well with you.

Bless you my child!
Old Man

Jake looked up at Christian after reading the letter and said, "Well what other surprises do you have for us?"

He looked over to Sherry and smiled. "Girl you have some splainen to do!"

Christian slid over with a cup of tea in his hand and said, "Well if we don't get going Jake will starve. Let me finish. The Clavis Ohrel we now know is buried in Peru. He raised the old skin chest high. The outline that I hold in my hands describes all the details that you will need in order to find the other key.

"Jake, Ieke has the part of the map that describes where to find the location of Clavis Ohrel. We allowed him to take the document before some of us knew he was off the reservation. Fortunately he only has a segment of the map because the Old Man knew that the copy Ieke took was incomplete, only part of the outline was provided.

"As usual, the Old Man was absolutely correct in that Ieke would use the knowledge selfishly. The Old Man made an exact duplicate of the lower right hand third of the document. The map and various descriptions located on the skin provide very precise background. Trust me when I say, it literally can change the world. Sherry has more information on the two Keys or Clavicularius as they are called. So Sherry why don't you complete the loop for me? A sliver of history might be helpful."

Sherry said, "I'm sure you're up to date on the terrible, miraculous and wonderful events that occurred in the early years of the mission. Most everyone knows that Cephas is the knight that the Maestro selected to lead the order after his death. You know Cephas was a tough guy. He was first given the Keys by the Maestro himself. You might be aware that he was also the guy who cut off the ear of a body guard when Maestro was arrested prior to his trial. It is said that Cephas was put to death by some of the same mob. They supposedly hung him from a cross upside down after he refused to give up the treasures. He wanted to die upside down, this was at his request!"

"I know the story but are you saying that the Keys really exit?" Jake asked.

"That is exactly what I am suggesting. The Clavicularius or the keys, as we call them, are real." Christian replied.

Sherry added, "Here's the kicker; Cephas's sword and the Keys, in the wrong hands, will create major chaos. If Ieke and his minions were to get all three items they would receive real supernatural power. Like power that can only be seen in fantasy books. Ieke knows that."

Christian said, "Fortunately for us, the piece of the map he has leads only to one of the three items. We don't believe that he has found any of the three yet, but he is very close. We think he is in the right spot. You are to go down to Peru to get the key back from Ieke. Then you are to search out the sword. The rest of the information is provided on the table so let's take a break and eat something. We can answer all the questions you might have at a later time."

The smell of Pizza filled the air. Mario's, just down the street was famous for its delicious and piping hot pizza. The fantastic story of lost Keys or Clavicularius as Christian described, was difficult for Jake to wrap his head around. Jake needed more information on the power of the artifacts and how that energy might be used. The answer to these and his many other questions would have to wait.

As usual he was hungry. Unabashedly he turned around and opened the large box and put two pieces on his plate. Sherry slowly opened the other box and put one piece of the vegetarian on her plate. Christian walked over, cut one slice in half and put that on his plate.

"You aren't hungry are you Jake?" He said as he turned and walked back to his chair.

"That's all we need to do tonight. I'll see you back here tomorrow. I am putting you up at the DuPont Circle Hotel, if that's acceptable, then we'll get together in the morning at seven sharp. See you guys later."

Christian slid the small crust in his mouth, grabbed his briefcase from behind the desk and walked out. It was as if the chill of the night was becoming their guest. Jake and Sherry sat looking at each other strangely. While still together, they felt alone in a large wooden cage of an office that was repelling them. Very little was said, the reality of their task was now alive and filling the room with a frosty and foreboding fog. It was time for them to leave.

8

WARNINGS AND ORDERS

Zoe's café was a stone's throw from DuPont Circle. It was a short walk from Christian's office. It felt small and cozy. The time-darkened wood paneling added to the homey touch. After a breakfast of dry toast, cereal, coffee and orange juice, Jake and Sherry hailed a taxi and returned to Christian's office. It was 7:00 AM. Christian was sitting in his large desk chair reading the Times. Sherry hopped across the room leaving Jake behind at the door. She sat on the other side of the desk facing Christian. Christian was already through his third newspaper.

Jake scanned the large opulently decorated office. He shook his head as he sat in the large leather arm chair situated on the left of the large Black Walnut desk.

He said, "What wonderful things do you have for us today? "Christian smiled as he peered through his reading glasses up at Jake over the newspaper.

Holding up a small disc he said, "Well my friends, today prepare to be amazed" He handed the DVD to Jake.

"This contains all the information you need for this particularly challenging assignment. We are sending you on a tour;

first to Lima, Peru and then depending on how things go, I think, it's on to central Italy. As I mentioned last night, Ieke Rollands is in the process of seeking centuries-old venerated and highly prized objects. As is his nature, he is also looking to sow as much discord and chaos as he can. I don't have to tell you that Rollands is bent on destruction. Jake you know he played us like a cello even as he orchestrated his half-baked plans. I know you have already determined that he is nothing more than a twit. Unfortunately I was late in coming to this conclusion."

"Okay so why aren't the normal authorities after him?" Jake asked.

Sherry replied, "Isn't it obvious, we have to maintain a low profile when we chase these types. I assume that his grave robbing is in a sense just like a cover. Am I right Chris?"

"Kind of, he intends to use the things he finds against us and in his interest. I know you were on to him early Jake. He was behind the misguided attempt on Sherry's life as well as the attempt to steal the large sums of money from the United States government; that we know. It is true that he took the oath of the Knights of St. John. I have to tell you that we were somewhat naïve in letting him go as far as he has gone. We are now paying for our caution. We waited too long for more evidence and he saw our restraint as a sign of weakness. That is par for the course with Ieke."

"You want us to go to Peru, find him, and retrieve from him the items he has or will discover shortly. That ought to be easy." Sherry said with a touch of sarcasm.

"By way of background," Christian continued, "nearly 2000 years ago when the Maestro gave Cephas the special Keys their power was immediate. The Clavicularius are the source of power for the Knights. It is believed that they enabled early users to perform many extraordinary acts, deeds and wonders seldom seen before.

"These, it is said, are used in coordination with a third item of similar power. Recall the story of the warriors that took the Maestro from the park outside Zion; well Cephas drew a sword and cut off the centurion's ear. Remember it was the Maestro who instructed Cephas in the use of the sword. A Chereb or double-edged sword is the third item. According to legend, it is to be used only under very special circumstances and in prescribed ways. It is like a GPS for the faithful. No one could use the sword until the work was finished."

"Wait a minute, Jake said, "I'm getting lost. Are we talking about the sword that Cephas used in the park or another sword?"

Christian continued, "There is no doubt that Cephas carried the sword and the Keys into battle. So it was, when two or three of these objects are used together, unimaginable power comes to those who believe. This belief in the power of the elements is like a switch that activates them.

One of the Keys is located in Peru. The other, along with Cephas' sword many believe is still somewhere in Italy. However there is some dispute about that. Sherry will be able to brief you on that. Right little lady?"

"That's right sir, I haven't told Jake everything yet. So now you get it Jake, right?" She replied.

Jake just smiled wryly as he looked back at Sherry with a sparkle in his dark eyes.

"Your job is to go to Peru, get the key and return with it to Italy so that the Keys and the sword may be brought together again. The DVD that I gave you will introduce you and Sherry to all the information that you need in order to accomplish your task. It's very important that you not let on to anyone what your mission is. It's our belief that Ieke will be looking for you and would do anything to prevent you from obtaining the Keys. I hope that you can get on the move as soon as possible I'll be looking forward to hearing from you and to your success."

Jake sat for a moment; clearly he was in deep thought.

He began, "I have a couple of problems. First, hasn't Sherry suffered enough? She is not at full strength and still suffers with some muscle weakness. I can do this on my own and surely Old Man and I can get it done. Secondly why send us south? We could go to Italy now and some others could do the trap line in Peru."

"Sherry, what do you think about this?" Christian asked.

Sherry sat quietly for a moment and then replied, "I assume that I would be doing testing and technical surveillance and will not be directly involved in the ground work. Is that correct?"

"That is correct," Christian nodded.

"As such I would be in little danger throughout the project. Is that accurate?" Sherry asked.

"You have it right," Christian responded.

"I guess what you want me to share with Jake will answer his question" Sherry said.

"You've got it kid, "he responded.

Jake looked at Sherry and said, "I know this is something you really have do, but I— had to ask!"

"Yes you did."

Jake, having decided long ago that he was in for the long hall, said, "Then I guess it's time to get to it."

He picked up the DVD instruction packet and the other information Christian provided and without another word, he and Sherry scooted out the door and on their way.

9

THE ROAD AGAIN

It was nearly five in the evening when Jake and Sherry walked onto the plane at Reagan National Airport. Inside the Boeing 757 they sat down in row twenty seven, seats b and c. It was a short two-hour Delta flight from Reagan National to Atlanta.

While in the air the plane leveled off at about thirty thousand feet. As the plane began to slow to a cruise Jake turned to Sherry with his head tilted slightly down and to the left.

"There is something about this trip you haven't told me, isn't there?" he asked.

Sherry turned her head, looked at those seated behind and scanned those in front of her. In the seat ahead of them were a couple both looking at their infant child who slept in her mother's lap. Scrunched into the window next to the mother was a small twenty something who looked as if he has just eaten a sour grape. There was no one in the window seat next to Sherry.

After another quick survey of the area, she bent over and pulled her small backpack from under the seat in front of her. As she placed the bag on her lap she pulled out a small pouch from her pack. She loosened the string at the top of the small purple purse, it began to open. As it did, it revealed a bracelet or cuff. It immediately caught and amplified the light. It shown so brightly that Jake squinted as he looked down intently. She entirely removed the bracelet from the bag. It seemed to enhance the rays of sun that streamed in from the window. Jake widened his stare as she placed the cuff on his wrist.

The bracelet was made of what appeared to be gold and a bone or ivory material as well as assorted gems. He could feel heat move through his arm as the sparkling cuff touched his skin. It was strange and sensual all wrapped the same package. It almost hurt his wrist. It burned to a degree and yet at the same time seemed to warm and calm his entire body. He took it off and carefully laid it back in her lap.

"This thing is scary; what is it?" Jake asked.

"This is what we are after." Sherry whispered as she placed it back in her pack and slid it under the seat.

"We are fairly certain that there are two of these in existence. Together by now you know them to be the Clavicularius. The reason for the name is because it or should I say they literally give the wearer the power to free or enslave people."

She placed her finger over her lips, indicating that Jake should not ask the question that was now burning in his head. Instead of saying anything Jake just looked at Sherry with piercing eyes.

Who is this woman that I love and thought I knew? Jake pondered.

Sherry opened her lap-top computer and the screen automatically illuminated. She typed in, Mathew 16:19. Then Jake saw what appeared:

> "I will give you the keys of the kingdom of Heaven; whatever you bind on earth will be

bound in heaven, and whatever you loose on earth will be loosed in Heaven."

"This is one of the Cuffs that make up the Clavicularius; this pair is the real deal," she said.

Jake shuddered and felt his blood turn hot inside his skin as he began to think about what he read. The plane was pulling up to the gate in Atlanta before he uttered another word. As they walked down the ramp, Jake felt like he had a boulder in his throat.

Jake choked, "I am sure you will enlighten me shortly, you have to know you are psyching me out."

Sherry looked over to Jake and smiled as she touched his arm ever so gently. The trip through the international gates was uneventful other than the strange fascination with Jake's wrist. It was checked with a wand several times by an agent whose eyes widened as if she was hoping to find contraband. The same hand that not long before wore the cuff. The agent, for a final time closely examined Jake's wrist. Sherry slipped the Clavis on her wrist and moved her hand slowly in the agent's direction. The agent shook her head like she had just swallowed a sour tomato.

She said, "Are you sure you haven't had a surgery on this wrist or pins in it?"

Jake moved his head slowly to the side. After another trip through the scanner Jake and Sherry were cleared for Lima. Jake walked over to the gate waiting area and found two seats a long way from any other passengers.

"What is really going on here?" He asked.

Sherry sitting beside him rested her elbow on his knee. She looked the area over as if she were concerned that someone might listen in.

She began. "You know the Keys to the realm you read about?"

"Sure!" Jake replied.

"Well you were wearing one on your wrist earlier on the plane."

"You mean to tell me the keys that are talked about in the biography by Mathew?" Jake breathed back to Sherry.

"Well that is what they say," She said confidently. "You want to know what Ieke was doing in Peru the past few months. Well, he was looking for the Clavicularius, or as you now know, Keys. We have got to get to Ieke before he does himself and others a great deal of damage. These items can drive a person crazy if they are not used properly. You remember when I was in the cave?"

"Sure I do," Jake replied.

"Well it so happens that the cuff I now have, was given to me by Ariel."

"I remember what you said. You told me to follow Ariel," Jake continued.

"That's it." Sherry said, "Old Man knew the Clavis Ariel was there, but Ieke didn't. Old Man was always ahead of us, if you know what I mean. Fortunately I was guided by Ariel when I was imprisoned. Without Ariel, I would not have made it. I am pretty sure Old Man knew that too."

10

ROLLANDS IS DISAPPOINTED

Ann continued to share the details Clay had uncovered about Sherry's imprisonment in the cave in New Mexico. Fighting off her sleepiness Ruth tried to maintain focus. She knew some of what was being shared. But many details about Rollands had surprised and enlightened her. While she had been the reporter to bring Rollands and his self indulgent tendencies to light, she really had only limited information from her sources.

She asked, "So now we know for sure that Rollands was the guy behind Sherry's capture and confinement?"

Ann said, "No doubt about it; but Rollands was soon to discover that the map he had in his possession was only a portion of the original. He had taken it off the ground in Mesa Verde, New Mexico a long time earlier. He had thought that no one noticed him. The bad news for him was that the Old Man was well aware. The Old Man knew the smaller piece of the document did not provide close to the entire story. Besides that, the Old Man knew Ieke's plan. He had watched as Sherry was rescued from the valley at Mesa Verde."

Ruth asked, "So the Old Man was on to Rollands all along?"

"You bet, neither Christian nor Rollands noticed the Old Man pick up the larger piece of the map as it fell to the ground from Sherry's pocket when she was rushed into the plane before she was flown a thousand miles, then hospitalized in Seattle. She had torn the map in two." Ann said.

"This was during one of her desperate moments while she was imprisoned those dark days in the cave back in Mesa Verde. Ruth interjected.

"She knew the map was important and fortunately decided to tear it in two. She found the map and the Clavis in the prison cave which Rollands and Razier had left her. The Old Man knew that one of these Keys or Claves was now the rare treasure that Sherry held." Ann said.

"Do you mean that she wore the Clavis when she came out of the cave?" Ruth asked.

Not wanting to concede that she didn't know the answer Ann replied, "Most of the knights had no idea that for many centuries the Clavicularius was actually a pair of Keys entrusted to a select few guardians. This however, was just a small piece of the tale; a story that grew ever more complex and intriguing as more facts were discovered. It is true that the order of knights was splintering due, in large measure, to the destructive and deliberate actions of Ieke Rollands."

By now Ruth was blurry eyed and in a semiconscious state. Her head bobbed up and down in jerky motions. Suddenly the plane was jolted and slipped as it began to spiral downward. As it did, Ruth saw people places and things moving around her. The emergency lighting came on and the oxygen masks fell down from their containers. She sat pinned to the back of the seat; her anxiety getting ever stronger. Slowly a copy an article written by Clay Berry, the cub reporter for the Phoenix Sands, floated out of Ann's dislodged brief case. The case had been opened by the force of the jolt. She read the print as it slowly drifted around her. It said:

> "Jake Rader was a member of a secret order of underground operators, the Knights of St. John." She could barely make the entire sentence out as it floated by.

She was entranced as the article settled down onto her lap. She picked it up and began reading:

> "He and his new wife Sherry reported to Christian D. Poincy. Christian was the Sigma Knight located in DC. He was well connected and involved with the Washington insiders as he was in the international network of clandestine agents. Some say these knights are the same band that had been around for a thousand years. As with most powerful and secretive groups, rumors as well as contrasting and competing opinions exist. Whether saviors or self-aggrandizing fakers, the group is clearly at a crossroads. There is no fool-proof way of knowing the truth of it all."

The plane continued to spin, however Ruth sensed that the passengers seemed to be calm and quite oblivious to the pending disaster. Ruth thought it quite odd that there was no panic among the people. She, even though quite anxious, could not take her eyes off the paper. She was into the story that Ann weaved for her. And now she was actually seeing the documents. She just kept reading.

At one point she even asked herself, "Why am I reading this stuff when the plane might be destined to crash." She was hooked.

"In order to gain a more full understanding of the purpose of Jake's affiliates, we traced the locations of Jake and the others claiming to be part of the group. We found an article from the Seattle Star newspaper said that, 'Sherry Paul recruited Jake into the order before they were married. The two saw more than their share of action. While they were clearly lovers, they were also fellow warriors. They were highly-trained and well-skilled in ancient arts of self-defense.'

A slight smile appeared on Ruth's face as she realized the article was quoting her very story.

She read on, "It has been stated by close associates that they were disciplined to an 'extreme level' in mind, body and spirit."

Ruth felt s tap on her shoulder. Ann said, "I can tell I have been boring you right?

Ruth realized she had been nodding off again. She managed to say, "No, no, really I am interested."

Ann looked over her rims and said, "Do you know about Katy?"

Ruth pushed her head back into the cushion and said, "Tell me."

*I'm beat and I feel drousy.*Ruth thought.

Ann's voice faded away. Ruth thought she heard Katy Rader, Jake's daughter, from a distance very far away.

"Just before they left Sedona the last time they were seen, Dad was in our home planning. He slid from one side to the other in a large black leather chair in the living room. Normally he was a sandy haired version of Alfred E. Newman of Mad Magazine, except he had perfect teeth," Katy laughed.

"However, now he looked much different. Of course his body was chiseled and it was not a lot different than before—err, uh, and I guess very different from the cartoon character he somewhat resembled."

Ruth was stunned as she studied Katy. She was a dark brown haired knockout. She saw Katy in a room in the home in Sedona. Ruth noticed that Jake did not pay attention to Katy as she quietly read her book in the corner next to the bronze sculpture of a Native American woman holding a piece of corn. His hair had been dyed the night before to match hers. He had grown a beard and it too matched her hair color. She watched and chronicled much of Jake's behavior taking in every move he made.

Ruth clearly heard Katy say, "He was a man of action who did not spend a lot of time sitting. He just wouldn't be confined to a desk. He regularly interspersed pushups, abdominal exercises, one armed pull-ups and kettlebell swings as he completed his desk work. He added nearly 20 pounds of pure muscle to his body in less than a year. In addition to dying his hair, the added bulk made him nearly unrecognizable to those who may have known him just a few years earlier."

That doesn't surprise me, Ruth thought, *I learned that he was a hard worker at his job.*

Katy continued, "You know, Sherry changed also. She was blonde and wore blue contact lenses. Her hair was short and cut in a wedge. There was no evidence of her green eyes or that she was a brunette. He and Sherry regularly raced to the top of Bell Rock. It was a nearly-vertical piece of red earth not more than a mile from their home. They routinely jogged to the icon and then timed each other to the peak. It was a hard scramble up the sandstone face.

Sherry showed little evidence of the leg damage she sustained earlier. That was when she was confined in a cave and abused at the hands of renegades. Even before the ordeal she could not match the speed and agility that Jake now showed. She still could match many athletes in the difficult and somewhat dangerous trek."

Just then as the plane seemed to be suspended in midair, another article appeared hovering just over her head. She looked up and read.

"On that particular day, he did not plan a run with Sherry. He was in the main room of the house in an easy chair."

Katy asked, "Why can't we go for a walk?"

Katy now sitting next to Ruth said, "Dad said, 'Paperwork is important, I have to attend to it; even though I don't necessarily want to.'

He chose to work in as comfortable a place as he could when he was not exercising or working on self-defense skills."

Katy shed a tear as she related, "He regularly took Sam and me hiking in the hills just outside the house. He said, 'Ya know, chasing bad guys is a poor substitute for hiking in the hills or kicking the soccer ball with you two. I Love you. Today what is important however, is the paperwork.'"

Katy said, "Dad and Sherry were 'laying low' following their last mission."

Ruth saw a scrap of paper tucked into the pocket of the seat back. She pulled it out.

It said, "Christian sent regular updates and information. Scientific research, news and various philosophy pieces were contained in the material they had to know in order to be ready."

Ruth shook her head and looked twice at the pocket of the seat in front of her. Instead of safety instructions there was a laminated note.

It said "The kids knew that he and Sherry must not be bothered when they were 'working' and they generally honored the rule. His parents understood that he was doing important work and helped the kids to understand the situation. What his parents wanted to discuss but could not, were many specifics about the work."

Ruth heard Katy whisper in her ear, "Nanna told me she worried from time to time; especially early in the morning. Dad told me that if he went missing they could track his moves and his notes through contacts in Italy." She could not see Katy.

Katy seemed to be sitting in the seat beside Ruth. She whispered in her ear, "Dad was satisfied with the arrangement but it bothered him. He told me more than one time that he had not been the father he wanted to be. He could not be totally dedicated to his cause and to his family. This is what made him so upset and distracted as he so badly wanted to be the knight that he was and the person the others in the family just could not know."

11

A SCOUTING TRIP

Delta flight 683 left Atlanta on time. Jake and Sherry were seated in coach class along with a few hundred tourists, business persons, students and others. The plane was headed for various Central and South American destinations. In the cargo hold was Sherry's suitcase jammed with the most sophisticated monitoring and communications gadgets money could buy.

It made it through security screening after a team of security "experts" including TSA and American border agents conducted various chemical and physical inspection tests on two pieces of sensitive satellite and global positioning scanners.

Jake was thoroughly consumed by his book. It summarized the various textiles and gold and silver refining techniques used by the native Peruvian people during the pre and early post Columbian periods. As was typical for him, his mind revisited the strange knowledge he had been given about the Clavicularius, the Chereb and what it all meant.

Sherry watched Jake pore over the material. She couldn't help but smile as he read, tracking each word with his right index finger.

"Wow, you are really focused." Sherry said.

Jake had a serious deadpan look to his face. He looked like Clint Eastwood in "A Fist Full of Dollars."

"Well I have to admit your revelations made me realize the ends to which Ieke might go; especially since he most likely has very little money left. Thanks to you and I guess me. I suppose he is very desperate." Jake responded.

"I agree we are now dealing with desperation. You know that desperation breeds wild and sometimes crazy acts." Sherry suggested.

"That I know but I just can't imagine the things you have been telling me are true." Jake said.

"Believe it and prepare; that's what you can do." Sherry said.

Jake turned toward Sherry. "Did you know that the mummies in Peru were buried in a seated cross legged position?" He said.

Sherry looked at Jake with a half-smile, one eyebrow raised, "What does that have to do with Rollands, or, for that matter, our own plan to get the Clavis back to Italy?"

"Uh, well, I'm Just giving you another interesting tidbit from my steel vault of a mind." Jake said smiling.

With a cracking sound and without warning, the plane lurched to the right as it lost fifty feet in altitude.

After a long noiseless pause, the guy sitting across the aisle from Jake broke the silence.

He said, "Welcome to the Andes."

A few snickers were heard in the back sections which gave way to thunderous applause. The plane continued on without additional excitement. Thirty minutes later the plane was on the ground at the Jorge Chavez airport in Callao, Peru.

Jake and Sherry finished the walk down the long cold corridor of mainly concreate and stone. Sherry looked out across the sea of heads and said, "Look who's here."

Jake's countenance rose as his eyes made contact with the Old Man. His long, now pure-white hair flowed out from under his tattered brown cowboy hat. His white goatee never was impressive, now it sprouted just a few curled hairs; not enough to cover his face. Sherry danced over and hugged him as Jake smiled a wide cat-faced grin. There was something alluring or exciting and at the same time, calming about him. He released Sherry from his clutches and he turned to Jake.

He said, "It is genuinely great to see you again my young friends."

He grabbed Jake and pulled him into a strong bear hug. Jake felt a warm sense of security surround his soul.

The shuttle bobbed and bounded its way through the pothole ridden streets as Sherry, Jake and the Old Man scanned the wares of the hundreds of little store fronts, car-fixit shops and neighborhood cantinas.

Jake wondered; *how are we going to track down Ieke in this mass of over nine million people?*

The three arrived at the hotel not far from Kennedy Park. This and adjoining structures initiated a sharp contrast to the simple stores and village homes of the outlying areas. After a short stop at the front desk and a simple elevator ride, they arrived at their quarters. While not remarkable by North American standards, the hotel room provided a nice view of the city Pizarro loved. The room provided a partial view of the "cat park" as many locals called it.

"Tomorrow the real work begins." Jake said with a smile. The suitcase fell open as he slid it into the large closet.

"Be prepared," Sherry said, "we will be up to our eyes with the challenges shortly."

12

THE GOLDEN CLAVIS

Ruth was interested in and frankly, quite amazed by the massive background material Ann and her group had obtained. She was also re-engaging in the story of Jake and Sherry. Clearly she knew them well from her research into the Cedarvale incident. She really only saw them from the teaching and administrative view. But she was beginning to see a much bigger and more complex situation than she had imagined.

Ruth said, "Where is your knowledge of the painting and Rollands really coming from? It can't be that much from Katy–– she is so young."

Ann replied, "Much of the information regarding the painting was obtained from Jake's journal. I think the journal was fascinating. He wrote more than once about that and to be fair, it provided much of what we know. Mind you, most of the journal is trudging through Jake's total commitment to, you know, he was taken with Sherry. His writing included reflections on Rollands too."

Ruth added, "I think he always knew Rollands was up to no good. Jake saw Rollands as pure evil."

"As I said, he was very intrigued with the Villalpando painting and Rollands. The images in this historical piece moved him more at an emotional level than any written word might ever do; at least that is what he wrote. Sherry and he discussed this very work and its impact until the owls where hooting the night before they left for DC. Ann Said.

"Wait, how did they get so excited about the painting? Ruth asked.

"They had seen the original a few years back in Philadelphia, on a weekend trip from DC. Sherry remembered the piece because the master was one of the most renowned Mexican artists in history. Sherry was spellbound by Villalpando's choice of silky greens and blues for the antichrist. Elijah a major Jewish prophet and the Sultan, who was an Islamic icon, wear cloaks of a similar look but in reverse as they look on." Ann said.

"Why would he paint these two in matching cloaks of inverse image?" Ruth asked.

Ann said, "Are you asking me, I barely know an acrylic from oil. Although I have written many pieces on the French impressionists, ya know."

"I did not know that." Ruth said with a sprig of sarcasm.

"Sherry also wondered if the face of the antichrist and the Sultan were in fact the same." Ann said.

Ruth hadn't seen the painting but she had pictured the work in her mind. *Why might a painter compose two characters with the same face?* She thought.

Ruth surmised, "Jake was a bit of a romantic with a bit of attention disorder I think."

"Given a piece of artwork with this kind of impact why wouldn't his mind wander? He wrote in his journal that the picture of Saint Francis of Assisi doing battle with the forces of evil troubled him in his soul. He also wondered where the marks on Saint Francis's hands and feet came from. He couldn't resolve the conflict between good and evil on two sides of the painting." Ann said.

"Is it really that awful?" Ruth asked

"Not at all, actually for a work completed in the late 17th century it is grand," Ann uttered as she shook her head.

Ruth felt a tap on her shoulder. Her eyes snapped open and she looked over at Ann.

"Are you still with us," Ann was saying.

Attempting to hide her embarrassment, Ruth fumbled for her seat belt. She had nearly slipped off to sleep.

"Yes but I have to use the restroom." She said as she unbuckled the restraint, untangled her deer-like legs and slid into the aisle shaking her head.

She used the lavatory for necessary business and also to splash her face with water. She returned from the lavatory and sat again in her place.

"Boy that took about all the will power I had. That place is a mess and we are only less than an hour into the flight," Ruth said.

"Christian sent him the picture, that, I know!" Ann said with a power behind each word.

"I can just see Jake there sipping tea and jotting notes in his journal, but if he didn't write about it he probably had no answer." Ruth smiled.

"Okay, so why did Christian send Jake a painting of St. Francis anyway? He was a major hero in Italy but what, in heaven's name, did he have to do with Central or South America, let alone the weather?" Ruth asked.

"Patience my dear, patience," Ann said.

"What does that have to do with Rollands? What do the Antichrist and Elijah have to do with Jake and Sherry and their projects?" Ruth asked. Then continued "But we were talking about weather weren't we?"

Ann said, "Well we are not totally sure; but as I said, the work was done for the Franciscan Convent in Guatemala. Jake wrote that 'Sherry reminded me early in the morning before leaving for Washington DC, that these and other questions would be answered.' He could not help but jot down these thoughts because he was so stumbling drunk in love with Sherry."

The plane was flying smoothly again. It was traversing the land of a thousand lakes; Ruth glanced outside the cabin window. She thought she saw another "Chereb fog." It was denser than most formations. It was at the same time, brilliantly lit with rainbow-like colors. The light seemed to be generated from each particle; almost like that of a TV screen.

She thought she saw the form of a woman pass by the window. Her continence shown so brightly that it produced the effect of a spotlight. She seemed to be smiling. But she was more than a woman it was like a man and a woman combined— soft and beautiful and powerful and strong all mixed together. She, it was marvelous.

Ruth felt she heard, "This is htiafeurt and ssendoog."

Then she thought she saw a likeness of a man drift by and it said,"Jake kept a personal journal of his activities and his challenges. The special code which was nothing more than the first three letters of his social security number, the next two of my wife's and the last three of mine. He had given the code to us. It was accessible only after he had not made email entries for more than one week.

"The journal was written on his personal phone and sent in code to my computer. The codes were translated and printed out on a home printer and stored along with other information in a safe in the garage. My wife stored the access code in her safety deposit box, which she told the grandkids could be opened in the event of the grandmother's incapacitation."

This shocked Ruth to her core. She was wide-awake and was pretty well certain that she had been nodding off. She wondered whether she had dreamt about Katy, the strange figures outside the plane, the notes and the plane spinning out of control. Yet for a moment she thought it possibly had really happened.

"Na," she whispered to herself, "Clearly the plane is still flying and Ann was still talking and the cloud well..."

Ann was engaged in her theories about Ieke Rollands and certain rumors surrounding his activities. Ann pulled the blind on the window a little lower as she began to share her detailed understanding of Peru. It was as if she was worried that someone might overhear. Ruth just could not interrupt even though she felt that her "Dream," was real. Or at least it seemed so.

"Now in the Inca region, not far from Pisco, Rollands lorded-over another small group of diggers. They dug not far from Tambo, Colorado, an important stopping point on the Inca road. It was late in the afternoon. Are you familiar with the area?" Ann asked.

"Well not really, I know of the Pacaras region. It is on the coast not far from there. I read an article about the sea life ..." Ruth replied.

"Okay so anyway, the rate of work slowed to a snail's pace. Sweat poured off workers' heads and hands. It was sizzling hot and very muggy. Suddenly one of the Peruvian diggers started yelling. His words were filled with intensity and excitement.

While Razier had only a rudimentary knowledge of native Andean language, he felt the excitement." Ann said.

"So what did he do?" Ruth asked.

"He just watched and then he joined in. First everyone stood quite still and just stared and then nearly all the workers crammed closely into the large hole formed as rocks fell from the wall. On the back side of the wall through the dust emerged an underground room." Ann said.

"Filled with treasure I assume," Ruth added.

"Rollands pushed his way through the group to the front. Razier stood behind as Rollands tore and scraped at the ground. Rocks flew and dust filled this newly discovered portal. As he pried a large stone out of the wall, rocks and sand gave way. A large room was visible through the now quite expanded hole. Ieke shielded his eyes, protecting them from the dust rising from the pile of rubble. Through the cloud, he saw that the area contained boxes, many boxes."

"Boxes!" Ruth inquired, "Like cardboard boxes?"

"No, not at all," Ann replied, "Most of the rough planks that formerly made up the containers were almost totally disintegrated. Termites crawled about as they were dislodged from their tasks. There was a small steady stream of water.

"According to Kareem, 'water saturated' many of the boxes. This provided a stark contrast to the mostly dry and dusty cavern. An oppressive smell of rotting wood filled the air. Rollands scanned the area. Blackened tarnished metal was evident, as it protruded from many of the boxes. In the dark, it was possible to see glimmers of what appeared to be gold. This pulled Rollands in. He ducked under the broken beams and caved in boards resting on a large case on the back wall of the chamber."

13

THE MEGA LOAD

Digging in the Tambo area was more difficult than in the Valley of the Incas. For one thing, while there was water in the structure, the soil was quite rocky. The dust in the cave was oppressive and often contained amebas and other none living contaminants. Nobody wore masks or other breathing apparatus. Rollands, with bare hands, pried open the large case on which a decayed beam rested.

"We found the big one boys, the Clavis. This is what we've been working for." Rollands said as he single-handedly lifted up what appeared to be a bracelet or small cuff.

It shimmered in the dim light like nothing he had seen before. He directed Razier and others to return to the old house and bring packing cases. Men scurried up the tunnel. Soon the entire area was filled with men moving at break neck speed.

In all Razier brought out four cases alone, each the size of an apple crate. Two Peruvians carried larger boxes out of the long tunnel from the back of the newly opened room. 5200 pounds of various silver and gold and other items were pulled out of the room and displayed in the living room of the old shack that was connected to the dig site. Rollands was giddy, mumbling and laughing as he marched around like a drunken sailor holding the golden cuff.

"I have found the Clavis. I have got the power."

Razier and the others just stood and watched as Rollands danced like a child. He spun in circles kissed the bracelet and mumbled incoherently. After hours of digging and sifting through countless piles of dirt and sand it was evident that only one of the Cuffs was to be taken from the cave.

14

THE NEAR MISS

The Mariel hotel was a boutique in the heart of Mira Flores, a nice district in Lima. It was a short bus ride to the center of old Lima. The Old Man was knocking at the hotel room door at 5:30 AM.

Sherry answered with a sleepy, "Go away, find someone else to harass."

"Tell Jake to bring the disc," the Old Man said. "I will meet you downstairs in the restaurant in a few minutes. The coffee is hot."

"Okay, okay," Sherry said, "we will be there in just a few minutes."

As she headed in to brush her teeth, she met Jake rushing out of the shower.

"N I C E," she said as she looked him over with a long slow glance; taking just an instant to gaze at his chiseled and hardened abdomen. Jake reached out to Sherry as she dodged his fingers.

A few minutes later, Jake and Sherry joined the Old Man at the café downstairs. He was sitting there reading the paper.

"Okay here's the deal. The buzz on the street is that the crazy wild donkey made a discovery down on the Rio Pisco. But we need to make a stop just outside Cusco first. It seems that Rollands is out of control."

Jake replied, "So what's new?"

"We have a few stops and hundreds of miles to cover. I have hired a guide. Can you two be ready to move out by 7:00 AM?" The Old Man inquired.

Sherry laughed, "We were born ready."

"Grab your hats; it will be hot up there." The Old Man chuckled.

Jake finished the last egg and sausage filled tortilla as Sherry headed back to the room.

Back in the suite Sherry grabbed a leather bag and opened it. She pulled out a small black instrument. She pressed the red button on the top and on a small screen was a picture of the room below. She caught a glimpse of two figures sitting on what must have been the bed. She pushed another button on the side of the small thermos-sized metal box. An indicator light on the bottom of the screen indicated a fully charged battery.

She said to Jake, "we're ready the day is passing."

Moments later, the entire group, Jake, Sherry, the Old Man and their guide left the hotel, jumped into the car and headed south in an older Fiat 500. The driver drove the car through hour after hour of dusty pothole-covered streets. With each mile, the cramped quarters of the small car seemed even more unbearable for the occupants. After a few hours they passed through Cusco— used by the Inca as the main palace and the center of the Incan empire. The road was getting progressively narrower and more bumpy as they wound their way another hour through the mountains. A very few huts and small farms dotted the landscape.

They came to a stop a few hundred meters from the town square of Andahuaylillas which seemed like a small set of court yards. The guide inched the little car right up to an old shack. He jumped out of the car and motioned with his hand to follow. Sherry pulled her sonar-scope off the seat and exited the back door as the Old Man and Jake moved out ahead. As the group followed the guide into the shack, it was clear that the back side of the cabin trailed off into a tunnel.

The Old Man with rising tone and volume said, "This is where your buddy Ieke was working the past few weeks."

"You have got to be kidding, he is not my buddy." Jake responded.

"Maybe I am not talking to you," the Old Man laughed as he winked at Sherry.

Sherry tilted her head and said, "hey, hey, yeah!"

As they made their way into the large cavernous room at the end of the tunnel, Jake was the first to gage from the obvious odor of rotting human flesh. Sherry A few seconds later, Sherry tripped over what must have been human remains. She let out a small chirp. The light exposed now maggot covered bones and blackened pieces of flesh alongside old wooden boxes strewn about the area. The boxes did not seem to fare any better than the body.

Each was dismembered and discarded with little or no care; or thought for that matter. Wanting nothing more than to leave the dead undisturbed and to finish business, Sherry pulled out her infrared device and pointed it in the direction of the far wall. On the screen another larger chamber appeared. She motioned in that direction. Jake fixed his eyes on a now illuminated yellowish object lying on the top of one of the boxes.

"This is the other piece of the map," he proclaimed as he reached for the parchment.

The Old Man said "Let us have a look," as he and Sherry leaned closer. "Can you see here it shows the spot right on this crease and note the small X. What does it say?"

Sherry replied, "That is Clavis Ohrel. I think it means 'key of everlasting light' or something like that."

"How do you know that?" Jake asked.

"Well that's what I was explaining to you at the airport. These Keys have a long and very interesting history. Tradition has it that, for example, Paulo the story teller had the Keys and what is known as the Chereb pars Cephas when he cured the Gaelic man in Turkey and made him walk. You know the story. In fact, it is said that Paulo was taken by an angry crowd and pummeled by stones in Galicia.

"The Chereb was taken and eventually wound up in Peru with Pizarro. I am not sure about that because there was also tradition that Bernardone was given one Clavis by the Sultan of Egypt during the fifth crusade. Supposedly Bernardone had the Chereb when he returned from negotiating peace in the 13th century." Sherry said.

"Now isn't it possible that somehow Queen Isabella got her hands on it and gave it to the Knights of Santiago? That's what I read." Jake suggested.

"You know that she had roots going back to the Gaul in France and Turkey. So regardless if he got it in the crusades or he got it from those connected to Rome it does not matter. It is clear that the Knights of Santiago are historically rooted in the Gaul and to the Maestro through Rome." Sherry replied.

"You have got to be pulling my chain." Jake said.

"She isn't too far off, but let's see how this piece and the rest of the map you were given at Christian's match up. At least we know that Ieke was here. This confirms what we thought. He may have the Clavis Ohrel and if he does, he can cause a lot of harm to a lot of people. We need to track him down. Is there anything else in this dark place that can lead us to him?" The Old Man said.

"What about this?" The small man that was guiding the group said as he pointed to a small piece of paper attached to a mound with a small makeshift cross on top.

Sherry picked up the paper and began to read:

> "Here lies Juan Goodman, truly a good man. He was murdered by IR who says he is now headed to the Pisco River to find his Clavis Ohrel. If you have read and understand this you are in danger.
>
> Do what you must but please, heed my warning!"

KR

15

CHASE IS ON

Kareem climbed into the right hand side of the Bonanza V-tail aircraft as Ieke took his feet off the brakes. The small plane with split vertical stabilizers pulled onto the taxiway as a slight breeze blew from the south end of the field. The plane stopped short of the runway as a small regional jet dropped from the sky and onto the runway.

Picking up the radio transmitter in his left hand, Ieke In perfect Spanish said, "This is Oscar, Bravo, Romeo 666 requesting final directions for takeoff, have a nice day, over."

The jet turned off the runway and headed toward a private hanger a quarter mile away.

An emotionless voice on the speaker said, "Oscar, Bravo, Romeo 666 you are cleared for takeoff; have a nice day, over."

Kareem raised his head and said, "A heading of 042 should be good."

The little plane lurched as Ieke pushed the throttle forward. Kareem felt the pressure as his body was forced back into the seat. Showing no sign of effort, the plane jumped into the air. The peaks of the Andes suddenly showed their heads as the plane groaned under the weight of full fuel tanks and increasing altitude. Cutting a large circle, Ieke guided the plane higher and higher reaching just enough altitude to wind its way through the valleys below the massive mountains.

Ieke, still bizarre and hyperactive, was like a drug addict on a weeks-long binge. He laughed as he glanced at the bracelet he now wore on his wrist. The craft scooted barely a thousand feet above the ground. For a murderer and a double-dealing thug to act strange is not the point. He was like a two-year-old who has had too much candy.

"What is with you," Ieke laughed as he shook the gold ruby and bone bracelet at Kareem. Razier did not respond.

"Don't you understand Kareem, when we locate the Chereb we will have the same kind of power Pizarro and Alvarado had hundreds of years ago. We will be unstoppable. How do you think Pizarro conquered thousands of Inca warriors with just a few hundred men? It was with this Clavis and the sword, that's how?" He pointed to the cuff on his wrist as he talked.

He raised his fist revealing the bright light shining off the gold on his forearm.

Razier was not impressed; he was becoming more disgusted with each passing moment. "You know, if you dislike what we are doing you can leave at any time." Ieke demanded.

It's as if he was reading my thoughts, and he is stranger than ever. Besides you are off your rocker. What can I do? Jump, right here? I wonder how much gas it will take to get to Recife, Brazil. Razier reasoned as he sat quietly.

Ieke commented, "You don't have to worry; now the plane has plenty of capacity to fly over the Andes. We will make it to Recife in less than five hours. When I had the wing tanks added it gave us a one hundred gallon capacity. We will be fine. If you want to worry, the trip from Fernando de Noronha to Ascension Island will be up your alley. Now that will be a gut buster. If we fly slow and straight, it is nearly 1300 miles and we will land on fumes." He laughed with what was now becoming an irritating sound to Razier.

"That's why we took so little luggage and why I removed the back seats. If we don't make it we can swim to Saint Helena." Ieke mused.

Razier clinched his teeth as the overloaded speedy little plane bounced its way between the peaks and along the river valleys.

After crawling through the mountains, the aircraft was purring along over the large grassy plains of central Brazil.

While still sullen, Razier finally asked, "So what is this about the Clavis Ohrel and your obsession with it anyway?"

"It's simple," Ieke said, "when we find the Chereb we will be able to conquer the world literally. I can already feel the power coming from the Clavis."

"It's just a bracelet," Razier said, "How can bone and gold give you great power?"

"Let me break it down for you, you dimwit. You know the map that I stole from the cave where you stashed Sherry Paul?"

"You mean the vellum map we left down there by Cusco?" Razier clarified.

"Yes that very one. The map said at the bottom, that the Clavis Ohrel and the Chereb will give us the power to enslave and free anyone. That is why the Clavis and Chereb have been protected by the Knights of St. John since the fifth Crusade." Ieke said.

"Yes but I studied that document carefully before we left and along the torn edge, I remember the letters **RIUS**. In addition, I also saw at the bottom, along the same rough edge, the letters **REL,** just before the rest of the sentence you are quoting. In addition I remember the letters GIA below the REL." Razier added.

"So what are you trying to say?" Ieke asked.

"Well I think there is more to the map than what we had." Razier replied.

"Now why would there be more if the document was stored in a cave so long. Don't you think that I would know anyway, I have been a knight not you? Trust me, if there was more written on the map I would know. Besides I already feel the power." Ieke asserted.

The Recife airport was just becoming visible as the plane started to descend into the former Brazilian capital.

16

ON THE TRAIL

Late in the evening when they arrived back at the Mariel Hotel. Jake and Sherry headed back to the room. The Old Man left for the small waiting room. Moments later he was talking with his main contact, a tiny dark-skinned Peruvian man with a large grey streak right in front of his shoulder-length, jet-black hair. They sat on scratched and discolored leather and hard wood chairs.

They spoke in low tones. The Peruvian looked up and scanned the area every second or two––like a deer grazing in a small field. The conversation lasted less than five minutes.

"I'll see you here first thing tomorrow the Old Man said as he escorted the man dressed in black to the door. The Old Man took a piece of paper from the front desk and jotted a quick note. He dropped the note under Jake and Sherry's door before heading to his own bed.

The next morning the Old Man and the informant left the hotel and drove to Lima's central square. It was just a short walk from the parked car to the restaurant. Named the Cordano, it was a reminder of the French presence in the city of Lima in the 1800's. It was located on Pescaderia and Rastro De San Francisco streets.

On the way the Old Man led the informant into a gallery in the Franciscan Monastery. The Old Man paused for a while as he studied the series of murals depicting the life of Saint Francis.

"Why stop here? I want to eat." The informant said.

"You see in this scene Saint Francis is meeting with the Sultan. It is well documented. Okay let's go," the Old Man said.

The small native man just shook his head and followed. The restaurant was at the end of the next block. They sat down at the old wooden table.

"I have been following Ieke Rollands and Kareem Razier for months. Ieke and Kareem employed a large number of Peruvian natives to help ransack ancient burial sites and caves that were found to be containing treasure of unknown value. These treasure caves are scattered throughout the River Valleys to the east and south of Lima. It is interesting that they were seen in the Monastery before they left Lima." The dark-haired Peruvian said.

"Do you know their whereabouts now?" the Old Man asked.

"Well I am not sure but they are moving around a lot. I think they were down near Pisco. My friend at the airport told me they left in a small plane a few days ago." The informant said.

"That's good enough; we will check the story out." The Old Man said.

He dropped a few Nuevo sols on the table as he headed out. The Old Man walked with a bounce in his step as he left the small café. He headed down Pescaderia toward the old presidential palace.

"Great news," the Old Man said as he climbed into the back passenger's seat of the tiny old Fiat that waited on the old parade grounds just below the steps of the Cathedral. There he rejoined, Sherry and Jake. They had hired the driver and car for transport during their stay. They had already checked out of the hotel and were packed and ready to go.

"We are off to Europe. It seems that Rollands and another passenger presumably Razier, filed a flight plan to Recife, Brazil just two days ago. According to my friend from Peru, they carried a large wooden trunk with pounds of gold and rare artifacts. We are lucky that Ieke made no friends with the locals here. They have been very willing to talk."

Jake turned his head to the back seat and interjected, "Good work my friend, are we going directly to the airport?"

"As you say," the Old Man replied as he asked in Spanish to drop them off at the airport. It was located just outside Lima in the city of Callao.

The traffic was congested; it took nearly an hour to get to the terminal. Even before the car came to a complete stop Sherry, Jake and the Old Man made a beeline for the control tower as the driver waited in the car. A twenty dollar bill in US currency was all that was needed to secure from the air traffic controller a copy of the monthly flight logs and other needed information.

"Here it is," the Old Man said. "They flew out two days ago in a Beech Bonanza; Loaded with wooden boxes."

Sherry suggested, "I bet I know where they are headed."

"Enlighten us," Jake said with a smile.

"Well," Sherry said, "if Rollands really does have the Clavis Ohrel then he is headed for Rome. You know what's housed just a few yards from the Spanish steps, don't you?"

Jake looked at her with questioning eyes while the Old Man turned to Jake. "It is believed that at the headquarters of the Knights of St. John in Rome there is a complete library of documents tracing the history of the Clavicularius and the Chereb. If Rollands is headed there he must know that he only holds piece of the puzzle."

"Then, why would Rollands head to Rome?" Jake inquired.

The Old Man continued, "As the story goes, Paulo traveled to Galicia to teach kindness, healing and hope and his teaching was witnessed by many people. These Celts, Gaul's or Galician's or whatever they were commonly called, lived in what is now northern Turkey. As we discussed he was aided by the power of the Clavicularius and Chereb. Sherry you have rightly told the story that these instruments were taken from him as he was savagely beaten with rocks in what is now a northern province. They robbed him of everything. Other accounts suggest he rebuffed the attack and then made his way back to Jerusalem."

"So are we agreed that when the Chereb turned up in the new world, it may have been carried by Alvarado, who received it from the Count of Auvergne in central France. You know from the queen?" Sherry added.

"Wait a minute, I don't follow." Jake said, "How did Alonso Alvarado get this Chereb?"

"Most think that that one Clavis and the Chereb were returned to the holy lands during the crusades when the Grand Master of the Knights of St. John, Pierre Guerin de Montagu of Auvergne claimed to have the Chereb and Clavicularius as he assaulted the Saracens at Dalmatia. This was the same time Bernardone visited the Sultan al-Malik al-Kamal in 1219 AD. Francisco Bernardone, it is said, obtained the Clavis Ohrel, from the Sultan. People say it was taken out of the Church of the Holy Sepulcher in the final days when Jerusalem was overrun by the Ottomans." The Old Man shared.

"So the Clavis Ohrel may well have been retrieved from the 'Potter's Field,'" Sherry suggested.

"Wait a minute," Jake inserted, "are you saying that we are really chasing some first century weapons of mass destruction?"

"Well not really," the Old Man corrected, "the oral history on these is shrouded in a patchwork of strange and exotic tales. What is written is a subject that is still being debated."

"Anyway," he continued, "when Bernardone received the Clavis and an ivory horn along with other gifts, he returned to Assisi after working to secure a peace agreement ending the hostilities of the fifth crusade. He was secretly given the Clavis Ariel and the Chereb by Montagu. You see, this was part of the agreement; both sides would give up their items of power and control in return for peace. This is what it has always been about; understanding the power of the Clavicularius and the Chereb." The Old Man replied.

"Just a moment," Sherry said, "remind me who Montagu was."

Jake announced, "I remember that from my initiation. He was the Grand Master of the Knights of St. John. He was from Auvergne. That is now part of southwestern France. It makes sense to me, given the cultural connections. Just sounds right that if these items were taken from Paulo by the Gaul's in Turkey, they very well could have been transported back to France. It is possible that the Gaul's held them and then entrusted them to Montagu.

"I assume, because there was so much unrest between the Romans and the Galician's. I am sure you both know that Auvergne is a region in France with a lot of Celtic / Gaelic tribal history. It is very likely that those people, whatever you want to call them, were the decedents that nearly killed Paulo. He must have had the items. The society that existed in the Gaul tribes made it easy to assume the items made their way to

France. I think that is how Montagu might have gotten them. " Sherry added.

"Okay but they could very well have been the real story behind the crusades. It would have been just as possible that they were there waiting to be discovered right were the Maestro walked." Jake said.

"Very good," the Old Man continued, "anyway, it is said that the Sultan and Montagu entrusted the tools to Bernardone upon his promise that they would never be used to wage war; so you see these rare and powerful tools have been treasured for centuries. Francisco Bernardone remained true to his pledge to protect these gifts to the death."

"Okay," Jake said, "so what happened then?"

The Old Man said, "Upon returning to Assisi, Bernardone started building churches. I mean actually pounding nails or lashing poles or whatever they did. After his journey to the crusades, he was transformed. He became fanatical about his mission. Many people in Assisi were engaged in the projects outlined by Francisco Bernardone using the power of the Chereb and Clavicularius as instruments of peace.

As legend has it, in the year 1224 he raised the three items together into the air on the top of a mount Alverna not far from Assisi. At that very moment there was so much power and positive energy swirling around him that he was permanently scarred in the hands and feet by the transmitted power.

A witness grabbed him and hugged him in an attempt to rescue him from the swirl of light. The witness said the Clavicularius and the Chereb dropped to the ground and the energy show ended. However Bernardone, from that moment on, carried the marks on his hands, feet and on his ribs. I think he was scarred for life or something like that. One of the knights told me that that the energy housed in these relics is so pure that people with evil inside burn to ash when confronted by the power." The Old Man said.

"You have got to be kidding me," Jake laughed.

"Well," the Old Man said, "believe it or not, Sherry holds one and Rollands claims to have the other Clavis."

Sherry said, "The map we pieced together, tells us that the Chereb is buried somewhere in Italy unless there is something we are missing. At a minimum the map makes a pretty clear indication of where the Chereb was six or seven hundred years ago, we know that."

"I thought these were just relics. Let's say that you are correct, that doesn't explain how." Jake said.

"These are matters you must explore for yourself. I can only tell you what I know to be true. You must do your own investigation." the Old Man said.

Sherry replied, "Let's get over there and we shall find out."

"Alvarado got control of them and took them to the new world. That is why you got your Clavis. It came from here." Jake said.

The car pulled up to the airport in Callao. There was the normal congestion at the terminal.

Jake got out of the car ahead of the others. He said, "I will walk up ahead and meet the two of you at the ticket counter."

It took a few minutes to get to the departure zone. As they exited the car the crowd grew larger and they began to feel the excitement of the chase.

17

WILD BLUE YONDER

The café was on the bottom floor of a quaint little bed and breakfast across from St. Paul's church in Olinda, Brazil. The establishment was full of tourists. Unnoticed by the other guests, Ieke and Kareem were sitting at a small round table overlooking the postage-stamp-like park and the steps of the church.

The sun was just beginning to warm the path that led from the chapel to the outdoor patio where they were seated. As it continued its daily march, the sun's light danced on the surface of the table. Normally Kareem would have welcomed the chance to be sitting in such a beautiful setting. At this time in his life the sun's light gave him no joy and neither did his environment.

He drew in a long slow breath as he thought about the trail he and Ieke were on. With fear and sadness in his heart, he slowly shook his head as he seriously considered the deeds for which he someday would account. As he picked at the juice-filled steak he realized he had lost his appetite. Kareem slowly pushed his eggs back and forth across the plate. Ieke devoured the breakfast steak and took little notice of Kareem's despair. He pulled out a cigar the size of a large sausage and lit up.

Moments later he was surrounded by a large plume of white smoke.

He said, "Well, Hotshot, in a little over an hour you will be in for the ride of your life."

"What do you mean?" Razier asked.

"Let me give you the straight shot; the trip to Fernando De Noronha Island is a piece of cake. It is only a little over 300 miles. Then we fly to Ascension Royal Air Force Base. We have a total of 100 gallons of fuel when fully loaded. Our little trip to Ascension will be nearly 1300 miles. I figure our plane can make 1350 if we have a great tail wind."

"So what's the problem?" Razier asked now sporting a half-smile.

"The problem my friend, is that the weather station is predicting a wind change tomorrow. What do you think that means for us?"

"I get the picture," Razier added.

"Yeah, we crash into the ocean off Saint Helena never to be found." Ieke quipped as he picked up the small cup of cappuccino and slowly drained the last few drips. He let out a laugh that was so loud that a young couple, walking in the park turned and looked over in the direction of the café patio before continuing on their way. He took a few tiny puffs on the cigar.

"We had better get a move on," Ieke said as he threw down 25 real, just enough money to cover the cost of the two breakfasts. Kareem stood slowly as he glanced down at the half-eaten breakfast and untouched orange juice.

The cab ride to the airport was a little more than 15 minutes. While Ieke and the driver bantered back and forth about who was going to win the world cup, Kareem Razier sat in stone cold silence. The cab stopped close by a small private runway. Ieke threw a few extra Brazilian Real at the driver. As he and Razier walked to the plane, Razier noticed how small and unsubstantial the aircraft really was. Kareem climbed in and fastened his seatbelt; Ieke was already feathering the prop pitch controls in and out. Ieke was testing the magnetos when Razier noticed how hot and desolate the runway appeared. The surreal waves of heat were now quite visible as they emerged from the hard, hot surface.

The noise of the engine droned on as the Bonanza sprang forward down the runway. Within seconds, the plane jumped into the air on a southeasterly course.

"Hey, Hotshot," Ieke said, "we are off and there is no turning back. Next stop Gov. Carlos Wilson Airport. It is a short hop. The trip after that will be the nail biter."

Kareem did not reply. He was focused on the blue and white waves glistening on the water. As the small plane continued its climb, he noticed far below, a line of nearly a hundred porpoises seemed to be on a chase. The string of aquatic mammals covered nearly a mile of water. Kareem was entranced by the beauty of the dark sleek hunters as they moved so effortlessly through the blue-green water in the endless dance of life.

He wondered, *are they just playing or are they chasing food?*

A little over two hours later the plane landed at Gov. Carlos Wilson airport.

"We are as far east as Brazil goes," Ieke laughed.

Two men wheeled portable air and fuel tanks attached to wheels over to the plane. Razier looked around at the isolated strip that looked as much like a cattle ranch as it did a makeshift airfield. Within a few minutes Ieke was back inside the plane and the engine was again roaring.

"I had them fill it to the brim. I just hope it was enough," Ieke said, "I just hope it's enough, let's go."

Soon the small Beechcraft was airborne heading due east.

"You were kidding about barely making it to Saint Helena, weren't you?" Razier asked. He could feel his heart pounding as he pondered what Ieke had told him earlier.

"Well, Hotshot," Rollands said after a moment, "we have a good tail wind right now but who knows what will happen in a few hours. I suggest you sit back and enjoy the trip. We have a long ride ahead and a lot of water to look at. Besides, if we don't make it, you have all those virgins at your disposal right?"

"That isn't something I prefer to joke about. Besides I have a whole lot of livin' to do before I worry about the afterlife." Kareem said.

"Hey, lighten up, you are getting too edgy. What is it? Didn't you sleep well last night?"

"I don't think I can lighten up, we have been through a lot and frankly I have seen and done stuff that is getting harder to face all the time." Ieke smirked as he pushed the control stick forward an inch or two.

The noise of the engine made communication difficult even with the head phones and internal intercom system. Razier wondered whether or not he should have been so frank with Rollands. Kareem had been a friend of Rollands a long time and they had been in a lot of scrapes together. However, the reality of the mission and the acts he witnessed were beginning to stress Razier. He was changing.

18

RACE TO ITALY

The Old Man was already at the gate as Jake and Sherry walked up. He was sporting the subtle yet contagious smile he was normally wearing. They planned to fly to Atlanta and then catch a direct flight to Rome. They knew that they were a few days behind Ieke and Razier but they also knew that a jet crossing would be far faster than crossing the Atlantic inside a small single engine plane.

In fact Jake remembered that Christian told him there were doubts that Rollands and Razier might make it at all. According to Christian, there were more than one, 1000 mile or longer legs required. That was if Rollands was planning to make it all the way to Europe.

The Old Man said to Sherry, "I talked directly to an informant who spoke to the mechanic. He told me they worked on Ieke's plane almost a month. He said he altered craft so that the capacity of the Bonanza, with wingtip tanks, is 100 gallons plus or minus. This will give them the chance to make the 1300 mile trip to Wide-Awake Field on Ascension. It still will be a very risky deal. The flight might take over nine hours assuming favorable conditions."

As Jake replayed the conversation in his head, he wondered what the Old Man meant. *What are favorable conditions for a small plane?*

They took a seat in the waiting area and Jake asked the Old Man, "What are the odds of Ieke and Razier making the jump to Ascension?"

The Old Man said, "You know I don't wager, that is not my cup of tea, you ought to ask your bride, she is the math whiz."

Smiling Jake turned to Sherry and inquired, "What are the chances of Ieke and Razier making it to Ascension?"

"Well," Sherry said, "that depends on wind direction, speed and cruising altitude, plus a few other variables. If what we are hearing is correct, it is possible, but I would not want to take the risk."

"I guess they have no other alternative if they want to get the Chereb. They must know that we are on their tail by now. Ieke has a large network of former military and clandestine fans. Some are probably reporting on our activities now." Jake surmised.

Sherry continued, "Ieke probably knows that his mug is by on every security network in the US and much of Europe."

"Yeah, they have to get to Italy before they are safe. I know Ieke is still protected by the Knights of St. John. I understand that Chris and others have informed the leaders in Italy and on Malta that Ieke, if he survives, has a lot of questions to answer." Sherry said.

As they made their way onto the jet-way, Jake was busy assessing the various possible courses of action that Ieke might be inclined to follow. He was sure that Rollands and Razier were at least a week behind them. That is, if they did in fact, take the risk of attempting the Atlantic crossing in the Beechcraft. If they jumped a ship in Recife, Brazil it would take nearly a month. Meanwhile Sherry and the Old Man would have a great deal of homework to do. As Jake thought, the to-do list grew longer by the moment.

For reasons unknown to Jake, he began to think about his daughter Katy. He remembered she was sobbing. He got up, walked over to her and gently touched her shoulder.

"Are you okay?" He asked.

She just shook her head. A slight twinge of guilt rushed through his head as he was still looking down at the cow-hide foot-rest where a map of central Italy was opened. It was part of a set materials coming from Washington DC. He stared intently at the map. He knew once the real work began there would be little time for maps and such. He expected to be sent back into the field shortly. He also understood and yet dreaded that he and Sherry would be called back without as much as a moment's notice. He was sad they had to leave the kids with grandparents for possibly a few months or even longer.

He was plotting distances and analyzing topography on maps of Italy.

Jake felt as if he heard Katy ask, "Why are you so sad?"

Then he smiled, "My mind was just wandering. I think sometimes I can't focus because I can only share these secrets with Sherry."

Katy knew he wanted to provide his mom and dad, and his kids, with the details of his work; but he knew he was silent for everyone's good. Adding to his problems, his brain was overloaded with details and questions.

Katy replied, "I don't blame you though; I know that you have to keep his work a secret from us and the grandparents."

Jake well understood the whys and wherefores. He also knew this secrecy was for the safety and security of his parents and all. This was a lot of what made him feel that he was sagging under the weight of the facts and figures.

Returning from his short day dream Jake knew they had to get to the headquarters in Rome and spend time studying the possible locations of the Chereb. Sherry had made it clear to Jake that they would likely end up in northern Perugia. In addition to Sherry's lessons from history, she reminded Jake that in her considered opinion the facts pointed to that area. At least that is what was indicated on the map they possessed. The plane filled with business people and vacationers took off. As it did Jake thought about the city they were leaving. He regretted that they didn't spend more time in Lima. He wished also that it might have been under different circumstances. It seemed like such a vibrant city and the people seemed so kind. As the plane headed out over the Andes it bounced and lurched reacting to the winds disrupted by the Andes. The mountains with the jagged peaks glistened in the bright sun as Sherry gazed at their grandeur.

19

THE NEAR MISS

The small plane groaned as it slowly lifted off the runway headed east over the Atlantic. Razier gritted his teeth and squeezed hard on the leather handle in front of him. It seemed as though the plane would not achieve flying altitude.

Rollands glanced over like he was reading Raziers mind.

He said, "Hey Hotshot, we are lucky the helping winds are 40 knots aloft. That will make it much more likely that we will make our destination. In addition I am feeling lucky today, do you feel it?"

Razier did not respond as he locked his gaze on the water below. He smiled as he looked down at the clear blue waves. The four seater plane flew on as the engine rumbled in the background. After they were in the air for hours, Razier was lost in his own thoughts. Ieke was busy adjusting the fuel mixture to insure maximum range but Kareem took little note. He was still thinking about his predicament and how, if ever, he might escape.

After the hours of silence Razier finally asked, "So what is the big deal anyway? Are we just going to be hiding out, or on the run or what?"

Ieke replied, "Don't you get it, if I get that Chereb, we can change the course of history. We will be like Pizarro was in Peru. We might even be able to take over a small country or two. I have a small army set up in Italy. You will be one of my main lieutenants. You will have more money, power and prestige than you have ever imagined.

The only people who can stop us are Chris, Jake and Sherry. You see, when you imprisoned Sherry in the cave you couldn't know that she would discover the only existing map to the Chereb. When we flew her back to Seattle she had the map hidden in her pants. Before I discovered the map I thought the Chereb was hidden in Peru; but now I am convinced it has to be in Italy. If we find the sword we control unimaginable power, not to mention the wealth it will also bring. Come on I know you are smarter than that. You know exactly what we are doing right?"

Razier did not reply his mind had faded into a fog. Slowly the twinkling of the sun's rays, reflecting off the water and increasing the temperature in the cabin, caused Razier to drift off to sleep. As he slept, Razier was transported back to the small village in Iraq where he was raised. He recalled the commitment and dedication his father and the others had to God; whom they prayed to five times a day. He left his home, his family and all that, to go to the United States. He taught school as an economics teacher rather than return to his country as an engineer. He was really and truly a mathematician. He was radicalized in the United States by the now convicted criminal Carlos Castilano, who disdained the decadent and childish lifestyle the Americans, lived.

The rays of the sun shone brightly through the window. They warmed Raziers face made him sleepy. As he drifted in and out, he questioned the choices he had made.

Do I really want to be aligned with this man?

He was fully aware that Rollands, who was in the middle of the movement, was an American, a knight and a well-respected gentleman. Yet he was in so many ways evil. This was the truth that plagued Razier now; the reality that he was teamed up with and closely aligned to an evil, power-hungry madman.

As the engine droned on with mind-numbing regularity he found it difficult to withstand the hypnotic effects of the sun and whirling propeller.

As he dozed, Razier began to see confused images. Ieke Rollands, the man flying the plane next to him, slowly changed. At first Kareem saw scales form on Ieke's neck. Horrified, he watched as Ieke's head slowly transformed into the head of a snake. Razier recoiled and rubbed his eyes. In his dreamlike state, he looked the other way and he thought he saw his friends. He saw Carlos, who was, according to Rollands, due to be released from prison shortly. He had a similar reptilian appearance.

Are these guys serving Allah or are they leading me astray?

Slowly Rollands, Castilano, and their reptilian-like minions, led him into a pit of vipers. The snakes snapped at him. They hit him with huge fangs and his flesh turned to boils. He turned and looked back from where he came. A pure and radiant light began to shine through the hole where he entered the pit. Through the powerful light he barely made out the image of his father. His father was beckoning to him.

It was as if he was saying, "Come to me".

While frightened, Razier he was mostly confused. For in his dream he watched as his friends turned into monsters before his eyes while his very own father beckoned him to return. In his mind there was no resolution, just animal fear and terrible anxiety.

While he thought he knew what it meant that Ieke Rollands was part of the Knights of St. John, Razier saw Ieke's deeds; the things he did were anything but just. Ieke's actions were not what he saw coming from Sherry or Jake for that matter. He had seen both of them in action, at school and in other situations and they gave without taking. Ieke was not Godly, he was wrong. He took much more than he ever gave to anyone.

Suddenly he was awakened by the plane lurching to the left. It turned nearly 180 degrees and began to slip as it lost altitude.

Razier out of instinct yelled at Rollands, "What do ya think you're doing? "

Ieke did not respond. He fought hard to keep control of the plane as it continued to slip toward the ground.

Now panicking Razier yelled, "What is going on?"

Rollands laughed, "Well here we go."

Razier could now hear the engine sputtering. It cut out then ran again. As it regained power one last time. It struggled skyward then the plane plummeted sideways as the engine died again.

Rollands called out, "If I can keep'er on the side long enough I might force some gas into the carburetor. We might make it."

Razer looked out the window. The sea was getting closer. The plane continued to lose altitude. He noticed there was land and what looked to be a small airport, not more than a mile away.

20

JET TO EUROPE

The Sun was bright as it shone through the small half-shaded window of the plane. The slender dark haired stewardess dropped a meager lunch on the trays of the trio. It consisted of a small wheat sandwich containing a slice of tomato, a scrap of lettuce and ham with cheese. The applesauce was hidden in a sealed plastic container and the cookies looked more like shredded wheat biscuits than a dessert treat. The coffee and tomato juice were the best of the offerings.

Jake turned to Sherry seated next to him in the center seat and joked, "Well what do you expect from coach class?"

Sherry tilted her head slightly and replied, "Were you expecting first class?"

The Old Man turned from the window and added, "well it beats pinion nuts doesn't it youngster?"

Sherry snickered as Jake looked over and said, "Old Man you grew up on pinion nuts, I guess you would know wouldn't ya?"

The aircraft touched down late in the afternoon in Atlanta. Jake rushed down the jet way in order to get ahead of the crowd and to save a space in line at the customs counter.

They walked through customs pushing the large cart loaded with their bags. The last agent to greet them said, "Welcome home guys." Sherry smiled back as the Old Man and Jake took little notice.

There was a three-hour layover prior to boarding the L1011 to Munich. They planned a visit in Salzburg after arrival in Germany.

The Salzburg stop was intended to be one or two days of study. The group would fully acquaint themselves with the history of the Chereb pars Cephas and the Clavicularius. One question they wanted to answer was; where specifically and how did the Chereb end up back in Europe, if in fact it was not buried along with the Clavis Ohrel? What was now a certainty; Ieke Rollands had the Clavis in his possession.

The note found in the cave in Peru was clear, Ieke had a Clavis and he was *not* in possession of the Chereb pars Cephas. The portion of the vellum map was not clear as to where the Chereb was exactly. It might have been in Siena or possibly in the Pope's palace in Orvieto, Turni or Perugia. These were just speculations based upon rumor and oral history. The Old Man indicated that they might find the answers in Italy, but Jake did not feel certain.

The three letters on the map were clear. At least the "GIA," that is what the Old Man told them. That could have been part of the word Perugia. In Jake's mind it did not matter whether or not the map indicated the location, that part if Italy was a great place to start. After the Old Man copied the map, he could have inadvertently blotted out a section of the original. Jake reasoned that was all that made sense.

Sherry was pretty sure that he had done that intentionally; however, since Rollands had the corner piece of the map, it did not matter. He really had little if anything to go on. With the other cuff in Sherry's possession, they knew that Rollands would eventually turn his attention to them. Still Jake, Sherry and the Old Man were hoping that one of Caravaggio's masterpieces might well clear things up. That painting was in the hidden rooms of the Castle Festung Hollen Salzburg. Sherry and Jake recalled seeing it on their abbreviated honeymoon in one of the rooms. The drive from Munich to Salzburg was only a few hours and could serve as a respite before they would drive straight through to Siena, Perugia, Orvieto or wherever the trail might lead.

"Let's get some BBQ; what do ya think Old Man?" Jake said as they exited the Air France ticket counter.

"I think that would be great!" The Old Man responded.

Sherry gave Jake a cool stare salted with a dash of contempt.

"What?" Jake asked as they continued down the corridor. Sherry smiled. The group took a seat at the last available table overlooking the concourse taxiway.

They ordered sandwiches, not BBQ because there was no BBQ in the terminal. As they ate, the Old Man said, "Let's have a look at the map."

Sherry produced the vellum document. She carefully unrolled the material as she glanced around the room to see if anyone might be interested. The document was titled "The Maestro's Plan." It showed the continent of Europa as well as el Nuevo Mundo Sud.

The entire document was written in Spanish, except for the three items of interest to the group; the Chereb and Clavicularius. These were obviously Greek titles. As Jake supposed, one Clavis might be shown to be buried under the painting of St. Peter in the Church in Orvieto. Yet, that was what the entire map really provided. The map might have suggested the Chereb was located off their portion of map; at least a small line and the CH could be made out as it trailed off the worn edge of the hide.

"What do ya see on the map, Old Man?" Jake asked, "Does it say Siena, Umbria, or Perugia?"

Looking up from under his foggy glasses the Old Man said, "Well as you can see the map is quite frayed where it was folded and it is separating the letters at just that point. As I told you, I really think that it is P I A because Ieke was in Peru. Remember he was digging under St. Peters Church in Peru. The (I) could be part of the word river and the (A) part of Tambo. Notice how the letters are written slightly from north to south. I Think the Tambo River is what we see here in faded blue because the river does follow the pattern shown at the bottom of our map. See here Lima is clearly written below. If it were a G rather than P then we would have to assume that we would find leads in Perugia. Isn't it frustrating that the ques are not clear?"

"Then why stop in Salzburg?" Jake asked.

"Well for one thing, we have been told there is a painting in Salzburg that might clear it up. Also the specific location is said to be scraped into one of the walls in a hidden room above the cemetery at the Castle. I have actually seen the rooms when I last visited the cemetery. They can barely be made out when looking up at the stone wall from down at the cemetery."

Sherry said, "Yes I remember the rooms myself." The Old Man asserted.

"Sherry, don't you recall what the other piece said after you tore it in half when you were in the cave?" Jake asked.

"I don't recall much of those days; I was in survival mode. Had it not been for Ariel I would not be here today. You know, Ariel guided me to the Clavis and sustained me during my imprisonment." She replied.

She grabbed the document and carefully rolled it up. She tied it with a leather thong.

Moments later they boarded an L-1011 to Munich Germany. The jet landed at around 10:00 AM Munich time. The Old Man was awakened from his sleep.

He just opened his eyes, smiled and said, "Gutten tag freundin."

Sherry laughed as she grabbed her luggage from the overhead bin. Jake was already out of his seat waiting for the doors to open.

As they exited the airport customs section, a tall young blonde man with piercing blue eyes greeted them.

"I trust your flight went well?" He said as he motioned to the exit doors.

Sherry smiled and captured Jake in her gaze.

She said, "Ask Old Man here if he can provide you with all the details surrounding the Atlantic crossing."

The Old Man smiled with a half lip turned up.

As he glanced back at Sherry Jake asked. "How far is it to Salzburg from here?"

The young man replied, "We ought to be there by early afternoon. It is not far."

The group jumped into the late-model, white Mercedes Benz wagon and the young man headed the car out of the small lot in the front of the terminal. The ground, over which the road laid, gradually changed from flat grassy plains to rolling hills. These hills marked the entrance into Austria.

After about two hours they arrived in the center of the square just to the south of the Salsatch River. The classic Bavarian buildings betrayed the wealth and opulence of bygone eras. Jake focused his gaze on the Italian fountain in the square as he started for the now familiar entrance to the large doors that led to the lower sections of the Salzburg castle. The young man that drove the group to the square turned the wheel and headed out without a word.

"I don't know about you but I am famished." Jake said to Sherry as they scanned their quarters in the lower section of the old fortress.

"I'll go with Old Man and meet your back here in ten minutes. Can you order lunch?" Jake suggested.

"Already on it," Sherry said as she pulled on her skirt.

"By the way, have I mentioned how much I love you?" Jake said as he handed her a small pink rose he had purchased from the street vender on the way into the Castle. Sherry her day-pack down on the credenza, walked over, grabbed Jake by the sleeve and pulled him close.

She whispered, "Ich liber dich, very much Mr. Rader."

Jake pulled her closer still and as their lips met he felt the soft tickle of air pulsing from her cool red nose. He did not want the moment to end, as he slowly caressed her pink cheek.

Sherry finally stepped back and said, "Well aren't we passionate for this early in the afternoon."

Jake smiled as he walked out of the room.

Less than ten minutes later Jake and the Old Man sat down at a table of thinly-sliced ham rolls and various cheeses. Grapes and grapefruit slices reflected the sunlight as the three sipped at the large bowl-like cups of milky coffee.

21

DOWN AND BROKEN

Rollands laughed uncontrollably as the plane slipped sideways rapidly losing altitude. Razier was gritting his teeth. As the ocean came closer, suddenly the engine fired and the plane began to right itself. Razier swallowed a small drop of bile as he focused on the land in the distance. The plane leveled off at 1,500 feet above the surface of the water. As he turned his eyes to the left Razier noticed that the hand of the altimeter began to move slowly upward. As abruptly as the engine began to fire, it again began to sputter. The plane lost altitude for a second time in less than two minutes. This time it slid closer to the ocean more rapidly than before.

Rollands pushed the control stick forward and jammed his left pedal in until it touched the floor. As he did, the small runway of Ascension came into view above the water and not far from the rocks. The plane slipped to the right as the runway appeared a few feet below the plane. Razier was unable to control himself as he saw the pavement coming to him just outside the window on his side of the plane.

Time slowed in his mind, as he yelled, "God save us!"

At that very moment, Razier saw the wing begin to shudder as if it was loose. The tank affixed to the end of the wing hit the ground first. Sparks seemed to flow from the tank as the plane banged hard onto the right wheel. Razier's head snapped forward then back as the wing surface began to crease. The plane suddenly pitched to the left as the tail swung around in front of the nose. The twisting metal fabric screeched as the plane spun off the edge of the runway and down over the small ditch paralleling the right hand side of the pavement.

Then it was over. The plane stopped, still upright and in the gravel sitting between the few sprigs of grass on the infield.

"Hurry, get out," Rollands yelled.

Razier shouldered the door and it opened. He disengaged his seat belt and jumped out. From the corner of his eye he saw Rollands following close behind. They stopped about 100 feet from the plane. Steam billowed from the engine. The plane leaned to the right, as the obviously-damaged main gear, was bent to the left. Rollands laughed as Razier slowly smiled.

"Well, what did you think of that? Rollands finally asked.

Razier began laughing hysterically. Both men laughed as a jeep arrived with two men inside.

One of the men, an American Major, yelled, "Hey General Rollands, are you okay?"

"Well Hotshot, how the heck are ya? I haven't seen you in years. Look at you, last time I saw you, you were a first lieutenant." Rollands joked.

"Well sir, it has been a few years," the Major said. "Anyway, from the look of the Bonanza you are lucky to be here."

"We were lucky we didn't have to ditch in the Atlantic," Rollands said.

"This is Kareem Razier," Rollands said.

"Let's get you outta here," The Major said.

Rollands and Razier jumped into the back of the jeep as the staff sergeant drove them over to the terminal which looked more like a Quonset hut than an airport facility.

As they sat on the tarmac Rollands asked the major, "Hey can you get that wreck back over here and fix the mess we made of it?"

"We are already on it. Why don't you guys get some dinner in our fine restaurant over there and we will let you know what we can find out. See you in a few hours." The major said.

There were really minimal facilities on Wide-Awake field; the majority being military installations. Fortunately, with Rollands' history and service record there was no problem finding whatever he needed.

They sipped thick black coffee. Joked and smiled.

Razier asked, "Where do we stay tonight? It's nearly dark."

"Good question Hotshot, I think we will have to borrow a bedroll or something. By the way, we will be here a while, if ya know what I mean"

"I think I do." Razier responded.

Rollands flagged down a lady at the counter of the tired old eatery and after a short session of jokes, smiles and winks, he convinced her to get them some food.

Razier nibbled away at a dry corned beef sandwich as he watched the major walk into the room. The officer walked over to the table and sat down, with a cup of java in his hand.

"Well ya want the good news or the bad?" He said with a half-smile.

"Shoot," Rollands replied.

"Well we had our mechanics look the wreck over and the good news is that we think the wing and the tank are okay.

We can straighten the wing with minimal effort. You are lucky that the wing didn't fall off."

"What do ya mean?" Rollands asked.

"You should know that these older Bonanzas have a bit of a problem with wing bolts."

"And what is that?" Rollands asked.

"These planes have a little box where the bolts hold the wings on. The box is built right into the fuselage."

"What's wrong with that?" Rollands asked.

"The box is a water collector. Not a good thing for steel bolts. I assume that this plane spent time on the coast somewhere. Because three of the four bolts that hold the wings on were corroded nearly all the way through. The last one actually broke off. I can't believe you didn't lose a wing in the air."

Razier said, "That's what I saw as we landed. The wing kinda flexed just as the gas tank hit the ground."

"That's the other bad news; we are going to need a new wing tank bladder if you want to fly this buggy again."

"What other choice do we have?" Rollands asked.

"Well there are always the freighters," the major joked.

22

THE BIG SCOOP

Jake and Sherry met the Old Man in the rather dark hall of the castle. The small man wearing black glasses motioned from the far side of the room.

The Old Man took the lead, as the little guy with glasses gestured and ordered, "Come vith me." His high-pitched voice echoed off the grey stone walls and floor.

He led the group down a long, dimly lit, hall to a small conference room. In the center sat a large table and six chairs. A bespectacled fellow took a seat at the far end of the table away from the white screen that covered the far wall.

He began to speak in slow phrases with a thick Austrian accent. "I am to understand that vee are looking for the ancient Chereb pars Cephas. Now you know that this ees a matter of legend and I cannot confirm or deny vhat I know. I can tell you that your guide has asked me to share vith you vhat I know. This thing you follow is one that carries great danger and can contain great power. There are many examples of destruction and beauty I could give you."

Jake spoke up, "Old Man, did you arrange this meeting?"

"Dang right I did and you, my son, would do well to listen to every word."

Sherry sat down at the far side of the table. Her eyes widened as if they were being cranked tight when the Old Man spoke.

The European with glasses continued, "As I vas about to say, the chereb has a long history. It started off in a garden at the beginning of human history and continued in Jerusalem. You all vill remember that the night the Maestro was grabbed in the garden, Cephas cut off the ear of one of the men in the arresting party and the Maestro spoke famous words as he reminded Cephas.

'If you live by the sword you vill die by the sword.'

That sword and those vords are vhat ve are about to study. This is a matter of the greatest seriousness. You all are of the Knight and therefore you know of vhich I speak. Now before you on the screen you see a statue of Paulo. The statue is in Vatican City in Rome. Notice that Paulo in leaning on a svord. Vhy is this important?"

"Well, I suppose it is ironic because the statue is in St. Peter's square and he, Cephas is the one that had the sword in Gethsemane," Jake hypothesized.

"That's a good start," the bespectacled guy continued, "yet ve are sure that Peter had the Clavicularius and the Chereb in his possession at one time. To that there was no doubt. But vhy is he, Paulo, leaning on the svord?"

Jake reminded the group, "The sword is a symbol of and in reality, a source of power that is not known to this world. Remember the Chereb was in the hands of a centurion placed at the entrance of the Garden of Eden as the story goes. The Chereb is described in the Old Book as a flaming sword. As such it is said that it has two sharp edges. The powers to heal and to destroy are somehow embedded along the edges."

Sherry added, "Keep in mind it is said that one must have the Clavicularius and the Chereb to have the power, isn't that right? Okay now I get it. Elijah has the Chereb in the painting Saint Francis Defeats the Antichrist."

"Correct, spot on," the guide said, "vhat is a subject of doubt is vhether Paulo had the items vhen he vent to Lystra. The record is clear that Paulo traveled to Lystra and did as much good as Cephas. Lystra is vhere he healed a cripple. He vas beaten vith rocks there. To that there is no doubt. The rumors are that vhen the people beat him they took the Chereb and later it ended up in the hands of the Gauls. The Gaul's, it is said, vent back to Auvergne with the Chereb. That is how the Grand Master of the Knights came to have it in the fifth Crusade. You see, the Grand Master was from Auvergne."

Jake asked, "Now we are getting somewhere, but, what happened to the Chereb after it was taken back to Auvergne."

"You mean before the Crusades, yes. It looks like it vas used to change most of Europe. If you know your history, Rome and allies including the Gaul's or the Celtic culture, spread like you say wild horses through the continent and became predominate even, it vas said, all the vay to England." The guide instructed.

"If Montagu had had the Chereb during the fifth crusade on Damietta, then why didn't the knights prevail on the armies of the Sultan?" Sherry queried out loud.

"Vell that is vhere it gets interesting. It seemed that the Clavicularius and the Chereb vere separated upon Cephas' and Paulo's death. The Keys or Cuffs, as ve know them, vere hidden either by some of the friends of Cephas and Paulo or those enemies in power in Jerusalem. Because the next time the Clavicularius and Chereb showed up was in the fifth crusade. Now ve know that the Grand Master Montagu had the Chereb as it was the source of power of the Knights."

"Stop right there, just hold your hat; I thought all of the items must be together for real power. This is just what we have debated." Jake said.

"Thanks Gott," the guide said, "One of the knights discovered a Clavis as they were in the process of burying a pilgrim in the Potters' field. The Knights obtained the Potters' field from the Sultan as a place to bury the dead. The other, Clavis Ohrel, was not there."

"Wait a minute," Sherry said, "I am confused; are you saying that the Knights owned the field where Judas committed suicide and where the Jewish people buried non-Jews in Jerusalem centuries ago?"

"The field bought with the thirty pieces of silver?" Jake asked.

"That's vhat I am saying."

"Is that the field of blood they talk about?" Jake wondered.

"The very same!" The guide said.

"It's as if these items could pop up anywhere." Sherry said.

On the far end of the room sat the large projection screen. It was five feet wide by three feet high. Projected on the screen was a painting. The painting had an eerie feel. It was composed in a swirl of action and seemed to be lit from the top and center. The painting was in a classical style with St. Francis of Assisi in the center.

.

23

ONWARD AND UPWARD

Ann seemed to be able to discuss in intimate detail any aspect of the trip that Rollands and Razier were on. Ruth was for the most part more interested in the challenges that Jake, Sherry and the others faced. So as Ann talked, Ruth peppered her with questions. As time passed, minutes turned into hours.

"You see," Ann told Ruth, "Rollands and Razier spent nearly two weeks waiting for parts. Rollands was becoming more and more irritable. He was in continual arguments with shipping agents and suppliers. At one point Razier began to wonder if they really were going to have to take a freighter to Europe rather than fly. The major problem was their location. They were on a small almost uninhabited island off the coast of Africa; in the middle of the Atlantic Ocean. The phones worked only a few hours a day and to get the parts they needed for a fifties-vintage Beech Bonanza, it was nearly impossible.

"Rollands said to Razier," 'I wonder if this worthless artifact is the Clavis or just a curse rather than a treasure?'"

"Razier, at one point, reminded Rollands, 'merely possessing the object is not enough, it is about believing in the power and acting accordingly.'"

"To that, Rollands flew off in a rage. Razier determined not to suggest anything else regarding the Clavis Ohrel."

Now Ruth could see in her mind the action on the island. She looked on as if she were hiding there behind the old rusted steel door. Things changed when the major walked into the shack like hotel room they had called home during their stay on Wide-awake Island.

"I have good news," the major yelled as he stormed into the tiny room. The bird is ready to fly. We just had her up and she screams like a hawk."

"Well it's about time stud," Rollands grunted as he peered over the two day old New York Times he was reading.

"When can we get clearance to go?" He inquired.

"I think you guys can get outa here first thing tomorrow," the major responded.

A light rain sprayed the runway, as Rollands and Razier made their way to the rehabilitated Bonanza resting on the tarmac. As they crawled in, Razier shook his head, as a sense of foreboding hung over him, like a cold wet towel. He pulled the lightweight magnesium alloy door closed. While he realized that they were, in a few short hours to be in friendly territory, on the continent of Africa, he was plagued by his uneasy and ever-stranger relationship with Rollands. For all his bravado and external trappings of confidence, Rollands was, it seemed to Razier, nothing more than a pampered and paranoid child.

"Okay, I am beginning to understand what this is all about," Ruth said as she looked out at the patchwork polka-dots of circular green fields surrounded by tan colored earth that marked the great plains of the central United States. "But why was Razier part of the wrong-doing in the first place and how did Rollands get so far astray?"

"Well you see Rollands talked as if he cared about people, but for years Razier watched as Rollands used, then discarded, those whom he needed. Razier, while having spent most of his adult life in the Western world still retained the Muslim values he was taught as a child. Rollands strict disregard for God, or as Razier preferred to use, Allah, was wrong. Yet Razier had to be careful; for on the one hand Rollands now wore what at least seemed to be a powerful symbol if not a manifestation of God's power. Razier had seen Rollands change before his very eyes. Rollands now seemed to see right through everyone and he was able to manipulate and use people even more than he had before. It was like Rollands, having obtained the Clavis, was more frightening than ever. As Rollands feathered the throttle and the small plane began to move, Razier was trapped and he knew it."

"Well Hotshot, we are off to Monrovia, Timbuktu and then to Marrakesh. I bet you are glad to be headed back to your roots huh? Rollands asked.

It was as if Rollands was now baiting Razier.

Can he know my very thoughts? Razier wondered as he attempted to hide any external evidence of what he was thinking?

"I guess I am excited to be doing my final fare-thee-wells to this lifeless rock," Razier replied.

"Can you even imagine how rich and powerful you will be once we have the Chereb?" Rollands inquired.

As the plane banked and struggled higher it turned to the north. It was clear that the extra fuel was placing a burden on the engine.

Razier wanted to escape but he still was confined in a place he did not want to be.

Razier asked, "Why are you so sure we can find these items?"

"Because I have the map and I have the training. You see I am connected to the leaders of the knights and that gives me the privilege to speak with and quiz the highest levels of the organization. That's why you have to follow me. As you might wonder we on many occasions choose this as a topic of discussion and speculation. I have been planning this heist for years. I did not expect Sherry to be such a pesky little hornet, if you knew what I mean. Now she, Christian and Jake are what we have to worry about. Having worked with Sherry for over a year you must know her weaknesses?' Rollands wondered expecting a response."

"Now it's clear, I wrote about these events, but it was never clear to me how they fit with reality." Ruth declared.

"Well I can tell you that if I was thrown in a cave for months after the beating she took, I would not be here to talk about it." Ann said.

"She is the real deal, isn't she? Ruth asked.

"She is a tough one, but, she is also warm and kind." Ann granted.

"So do you think they would be on their trail?" Ruth questioned.

"I am sure they were; I am sure they were." Ann said.

"I would imagine they were one step ahead of them." Ruth suggested.

"In fact, I think Sherry, Jake and the others really got caught flat footed just when they thought they had everything in control." Ann said.

24

THE HARD ROAD

The room grew silent as those gathered reflected on the subject. While the work was clearly a late 17th century composition, it was not evident to Jake to what school it belonged or how it was related to the project in which they were currently engaged. The Old Man got out of his chair and raised his hand so as to block the light flowing from the projector. He slowly turned to the group.

"I've seen this picture before. It is a piece from the United States correct?" He asked.

"Well you are somevhat correct," the guide answered, "the painting is housed in the United States. To be clear, it resides in the Philadelphia Museum of Art."

"I knew it," the Old Man exclaimed. "I saw that years ago when Christian and I went to a conference on the essence of liberty. I always wondered why Christian made such a big deal of the painting."

"Well enlighten us then," Jake said. He had an obvious edge of frustration punctuating each his words. This was the same painting he studied in Sedona before they left.

"Okay," the man with glasses said, "ve need to cover some details first. Is that alright Old Man?"

"Let's get on with it," the Old Man replied as he sat back down.

"This is one of many oils commissioned for the 'Convento De San Francisco, Santiago de los Caballeros.' It vas painted by Cristo'bal de Villalpando, the famous Mexican artist in 1691 or 1692. It is our first example of Baroque art dealing with our topic. But vhy is it important to us?" The guide demanded.

Jake responded like a kindergartener answering his first question, "It's obvious, St. Frances is shown killing the leader of some enemies of the church."

"Okay Jake, but do you know who this leader is and who are the others supporting him in the background?" The guide asked.

Sherry suggested, "I have studied this with Jake. Plus Christian shared this masterpiece with us. It is titled St. Francis defeats the Antichrist. But do you not see that the faces of St. Francis the Antichrist and the Sultan are the same. Look here at the noses and eyebrows, even the mustache. But notice also that the cloak on the guy behind St. Francis and worn by the Sultan are reverse images. They suggest to me that the good and the bad are all the same. They are within us."

"Okay I see what you mean but what about the guy behind St. Francis; he looks different." Jake continued.

"Well, I happen to know this," the Old Man said, "the one behind Francis according to the experts, is Elijah. He carries the Chereb, you see it is flaming. I think the evil ones are recoiled by the Truth in the Chereb, as wielded by Elijah. Notice the poor native underneath the Feet of the Antichrist; he looks scared and is one of the downtrodden. That is so sad in my view."

"I see it now" Jake replied.

"Notice also on the foot of the one floating up on the left hand side of the painting, seems to be wearing a cuff, a Clavis if you will." Sherry observed.

"Okay," Jake said, "but I don't see another Clavis. Do You?"

"No," Sherry said, "but I heard the top of the painting is missing."

The Old Man turned to Jake and said, "Yes my young friend you are bringing up one of the mysteries of time. There are two Cuffs. Ieke does not yet have this information but he will learn in a day or so if I can be so bold as to suggest."

"Yes we have discussed this before but, does anyone know what type of head gear is worn by the guy to the left of the antichrist?" Jake inquired."

"It looks almost Jevish doesn't it?" The guy in glasses said.

"So," he said, "the importance of this piece is that it can be seen as a precise road map of the struggle onvich you are about to embark. I assure you it is a journey that is fraught vith danger and was not something of which can be achieved without peril. It was a conflict that goes beyond you. It involves at least three major religions and uses many people who are unaware. You see Villalpando put on canvas the details of your quest. The challenge is not just a physical test. It is very much a spiritual struggle."

Jake said, "I remember when we were in Peru we were introduced to the seduction of power when we studied the conquest of the Inca. Recall that a brother, one of the Knights of Santiago was with Pizarro as he conquered most of South America."

"The Chereb was there, as was the Clavis Ariel. Ve now know that the Clavis Ohrel vas also there. vhat you should have learned also is that things fell apart for Pizarro and our brother Knight Alvarado vhen they took on the actions of a pseudo Maestro. The conquistadores lost their vay and vere as it turns out overcome by their lust for power and their grotesque pride. That, I think is the main message that Villalpando vanted us to understand. Heed my varning; it may be the same for you."

"Now remember that Bernardone traveled to Spain in 1224 vith him he carried the Chereb and Cuffs to the City of Galicia. Now you can understand how the Knights of Santiago came in possession of the items. Remember that Bernardone paid a dear price as did Cephas and Paulo. They all died difficult deaths after possessing the items. So I say to you take care in their use and be careful to possess them if you are able and villing to pay the ultimate price. Yes even to your demise. Now I vant to show you a few more pieces of vork."

Next on the screen was a painting by Domenico Ghirlandaio completed in 1482, titled Trial by Fire before the Sultan. It was an image of a Fresco from Sassetti Chapel, Santa Trinita in Florence, Italy. It confirmed the meeting between Bernardone and the Sultan Muhammad al-Kamil. Jake jumped up from his chair and made a bee line for the screen.

"I see it," he said, "see on his right wrist a Clavis." Jake was pointing at the screen.

Sherry looked on intently. "Yes it was there, the white and red bracelet. It matches the one I am wearing. Well at least I think so."

Suddenly, projected on the screen, was another painting. It was a fresco from 1452 by Benozzo Gozzoli from a Convent outside Assisi.

"It clearly shows Bernardone with the Chereb in his hand before the Sultan," Jake exclaimed. His voice increased in pace and intensity.

"Yes," the guide said.

He took off his thick glasses, walked toward Jake and put his hand on his shoulder. He lowered the register of his voice.

"You now have seen a small fraction of the evidence. But I vant to remind you this is vhat Rollands and his rebels are after. They vill not stop until they control all the items. Sherry you are in danger just by the very fact that you have one Clavis."

"I am along for the long hall," Sherry said, "truth is what we are after and we are committed."

He continued; "None the less, bevare that although ve try, ve cannot protect you all. I fear that even as ve prepare, Rollands has sent his agents to track you down. Ve believe that the Chereb might be in Umbria. That is vhere Saint Francis is buried. Many of his artifacts are there and although the knights have done their best to keep the actual location secret ve fear that Rollands may have uncovered some idea of the vhereabouts. Know also vhat is vritten on a vall in this very castle: To find Bernardone and his vork is to find the Chereb.

I have a driver for you. Please take care and follow the vay of the Maestro. You vill travel to Castiglione in Umbria Italy vhere you can be watched over secure and safe. You vill be able to use it as your base camp. I vant you to remember that the cross you vear has eight points and those points must be followed alvays, be serving them when you possess the sacred objects. This eight pointed cross helps us remember the elements of the eight blessings the Maestro taught. Ve must know them, respond to them and demonstrate them as ve live. Good luck and God's speed to you."

25

FRIENDS AND COUNTRYMEN

While the winds were favorable the V-Tail was difficult to control. The heavy load of fuel coupled with the boxes of gold, silver and precious gems made the plane fly in a quite unmanageable way in the wind and rain. The little winged bird ballooned up and down as it fought to obtain cruising altitude. This leg of the trip to Monrovia was not dangerously long but the constant float upward and the corresponding drops caused Raziers stomach to churn.

As the roller coaster continued Razier noticed that the plane was on an easterly course on a line to Mecca. As such he took the opportunity to lean forward and to recite his regular prayer. Rollands took little note as his hands were full just keeping the plane with a mind of its own in the air. After nearly an hour of constant fighting the plane Rollands let out a sigh.

Razier asked, "Everything okay?"

"Okay, heck it's wonderful, what more can we ask for. We are loaded with goodies. We are out of reach of the Peruvian authorities and this little bull of a plane is finally calming down." Rollands exclaimed with a little extra bravado in his voice.

Feeling a bit more comfortable Razier asked, "Do you ever think of the life after this one?"

Rollands laughed and said, "You have got to be kidding me. This life is all there is. All this religious mumbo jumbo is for the weak in the head. You have got to know that, don't you?"

Razier asked, "You had to believe at one time, didn't you? You couldn't have been a Knight of St. John without a strong belief— er uh could you?"

"Listen kid, I know there are some freaky things that have happened with this Clavis and the Chereb but these artifacts just contain some technology or natural powers we can't see. Some say they are left over alien tools or something like that. But trust me, there is no master manipulator up here in the sky watching and meddling in our affairs. At least there is nothing better than I am. Look at all I have given you. I thought you were over that, Hotshot?"

"Well with all due respect, I have seen some freaky stuff with Sherry and I think there was something to it."

Rollands took his hand off the stick, raised his hand adorned by the Clavis and said, "If there is a God, strike me down right now."

At that very moment a bolt of lightning struck the left wing tip and a crack of thunder filled the cabin. The engine missed a few times and then continued. Raziers eyes were the size of fried eggs. After about thirty seconds, Rollands let out a large guttural laugh. Razier just stared straight ahead. Neither he nor Rollands spoke for the remainder of the trip. It was late afternoon when the plane smoothly touched down in Liberia.

The alarm in the dingy room started buzzing at precisely 6:00 AM. Rollands turned over like an old hound dog and made a few awkward stabs at the switch control on the top of the clock. Without further disruption the buzz went silent.

Rollands yelled at Razier in the other bed, "Let's get a move on Hotshot; we will fry if we don't get tracken."

It was a short drive from the dust covered hotel to the field. As they walked up to the plane, the fifties vintage gas truck was just arriving. It took less than ten minutes to refuel as Rollands pulled the caps off the wing bolt covers and checked for moisture. This was an added practice Ieke initiated after crashing into Wide-awake. After a turn of the prop and a few kicks of the tires they are off again. This time they headed to Timbuktu.

26

NEAR AND FAR

After receiving the details surrounding the mission, Jake, Sherry and the Old Man headed out for Perugia in the region of Umbria. The road trip required that they drive through the Alps. Skirting the major peaks and as they were nearly exhausted late in the day the car arrived in Castiglione Del Lago, the ancient Roman outpost where their armies were devastated in the battle of the second Punic war. It has been said that Hannibal and his horde conducted the largest and most effective ambush in the history of war. The battle location is at the north end of the lake within view of Castiglione which is located on the southwest side of the lake. The accommodations had already been arranged. Rooms were booked at the Albergo La Torre. The small hotel is situated in the heart of the village with unrestricted views of the lake.

Planning another ambush and hoping for a success like Hannibal, a small group of renegades were already in place at a small farmhouse just outside Castiglione near Lago Trasimeno. The lake forms the peninsula where Castiglione is built. Five friends of Rollands received word from Salzburg that Jake, Sherry the Old Man and a driver were headed south and would be passing the farmhouse where Rolland's people were headquartered by late evening.

Sal Selces, the leader of the five, was sitting at the simple pine table in the rundown, abandoned kitchen with the four others.

"Now here is the plan," he began, "the car they will be in is a black Chrysler 300 S. It should be easy to identify as it will be late in the afternoon."

He turned to a large man with heavy black eyebrows extending the entire ridge of his forehead. The eyebrows formed the base of a flat sloping cranium that was bald and misshapen.

"Dujas, you will take this radio and ride the bike two miles down the road. Your simple job is to let us know when the car passes your position."

"Got it boss!"

"The rest of us will stretch this roll of roofing nails across the road just as the car approaches. Got it?"

Sal looked around the table and watched heads nodding in agreement.

"Now, since it should be dark, the driver will not be able to see the nails or the plastic backing attached to the nails until it is too late. Be fast and pay attention right after the car is disabled by the nails we will give pursuit in the Toyota truck that we will leave running in the driveway. Make sure that all of you wear your hoods and cover your faces. Smash the windows of the car with your hammers and grab Sherry. She will be wearing the cuff on her right hand."

Remember the objective is to get the cuff. That is all. Once we retrieve the cuff we take off, pick up Dujas and head back toward Siena. That is it, short and simple. Any questions?" Sal looked around the group studying each man's eyes.

The three hour drive through the Alps was filled with steel-edged views of solid rock cliffs capped with snow covered peaks trimmed by conifer trees and manicured dwarf farms. The Granite Mountains glistened, sporting a cap of fresh unspoiled snow, a crown of splendid white cotton and Icy aqua topaz. The blue sky above outlined the giant rock faces setting them apart from the green valleys and diamond-like river below. The Old Man smiled as he felt the divine nature surrounding the sojourning band of friends. The light was beginning to fade at 5:00 PM when the driver pulled off the road at a gas stop and convenience center not far from Assisi.

"Looks like we will be in Castiglione before dark," the driver said as Jake pulled the door of car shut behind him.

"Enjoy it now!" the Old Man laughed, "Tomorrow the real work begins."

"What do you mean?" Jake asked. The car was just pulling back on the toll road.

"Well, tomorrow we head back to Assisi and possibly to Orvieto. There is a good chance we will find the Chereb."

"If things go well we will capture Rollands in the next few days," the Old Man said.

27

THE SIDE TRIP

Earlier that same morning Rollands and Razier touched down on a small remote landing strip outside Tripoli, Libya. After an uneventful flight to Timbuktu they refueled in Morocco. They spent nearly two days in Tripoli. By chance, Razier ran into an old friend who knew of a person that could fix the elevator cable on the plane.

The control wire was damaged during the lightning strike and was becoming dangerous. The high voltage, it appeared, cut through the skin of the plane and melted a small spot on the steel cable that over the course of the trip began to fray. That evening, Rollands went missing for a few hours. Razier was worn out from the constant irritating antics Rollands demonstrated. He sat in his small hotel chair and fell asleep. After close to an hour of undisturbed rest, Rollands returned.

"Hey you lazy rag head, I leave you alone for a few minutes and you fall asleep! Think you need a little nourishment to keep you going." Rollands announced.

"Well a little food would be good about now. "Any ideas?" Razier mumbled.

"Yeah, there is a little dive just down the street. We can walk." Rollands replied.

As Razier choked down a green mixture of rice, beans and who knows what else, Rollands announced that there was a change in plans.

"What do you mean plans have changed?" Razier asked as he poked at the soup like material in the bowl.

"We're going to Egypt prior to the flight to Rome. " Rollands said.

Not more than an hour later they were in the air again.

"I thought we were headed straight to Rome from here?" Razier questioned as they reached cruising altitude.

"I already told you, plans have changed." Rollands replied through a half clinched jaw.

"What have you heard from the guys in Perugia?" Razier inquired.

He was digging for more information.

Rollands just looked downward and to the right as he glanced over the top of his gold rimmed flight glasses; glasses that were dark and dingy. The plane rose above the smog and dust into the evening light. He held his gaze for what Razier felt could have been a minute.

"It is none of your concern, but things did not go as l planned." Rollands finally spit out.

"What do you mean, didn't go as planned?" Razier asked.

"We will discuss this later; right now I have more important things to consider. For one thing, I thought all along that the Chereb was hidden in Rome. Now I have been told it is somewhere else and the people that may know are the Copts in Egypt. It seems that when the remains of Markus were smuggled out of Alexandria by Venetian merchants in 828 AD his bones were not all that were taken. Some say that Cephas gave Markus the Chereb when they met together when Cephas was on his way to Rome before he was killed hanging upside down. The merchants hid the Chereb in the pork along with Markus' bones. I have to check it out at the hanging church and I need to stop by the library in Alexandrea. Anyway there is little doubt that the Copts know a lot about this stuff and we have to get after it." Rollands concluded.

"I know of the story," Razier said, "but my tradition suggests that in fact, the stuff that was taken from our people was done without the right. The bones were the remains of Alexander the Great and not Markus." Razier suggested.

"Well you are too stupid to understand all this anyway!" Rollands laughed.

Rollands glanced down at the handheld GPS and adjusted the flap for descent. Razier bit his lip as the plane descended like a feather and landed at a small airstrip not far from the old Farouk Palace.

The traffic in Alexandrea was normal as cars merged and swerved in and out, honking and making a patchwork of perpetual motion. It was a procession that from the air looked as though a mountain of ants just discovered a mound of sugar. The cab dropped the two off at the huge structure that contained many of the worlds' most sacred and prized books and manuscripts. They walked into the library and took the elevator to the third level which contained a large number of glass cubicles. It overlooked the massive open research area some thirty feet below. They walked into one of the glass rooms to the right of the main indexes. Within minutes Rollands and Razier were in the company of a dark skinned woman in her early thirties. She was slender and efficient looking.

"Kareem this is Anneke." Rollands started.

"It is a pleasure," Razier said as he greeted her with an outstretched hand.

Razier had read some of her works before. She was a world renowned expert on early Christian and Muslim history. She was educated by the world renowned experts on rare and obscure relics. Rollands worked with her when he was doing advanced research for project Enduring Freedom. He found her to be responsible and factual. She was the one that provided Rollands with the detailed understanding of the functions of Sunni and Shiite culture, a topic which he had written about extensively; a matter on which he had received his first star. Razier had read her work on the comparative aspects of Christian and Muslim disciplines.

Anneke asked, "Why don't you have a chair?" as she rolled out over the desk top, what appeared to be an ancient scroll.

"Gentlemen what we have here is a scroll that was contained in the same earthen jars as the Nag Hammadi texts. Some examples are the Gospel of Thomas and of Philip. Basically what it says is that Markus was given the Chereb by Cephas. See right here most of the words are still visible. Look closely; they say Markus kept the Chereb with him even unto death. Now in talking with our Copt friends, Markus was buried with the Chereb after he was dragged through the streets of Alexandrea by his neck until he died. We know that his bones were taken from Alexandrea and the Chereb must have been taken along with other items with which he was buried."

Razier said, "So we are looking at a part of a document that is nearly 2000 years old and was part of the original discovery."

"That is exactly what it was." She replied.

"Are you suggesting that we start our search in Venice rather than waste time and energy in Rome?" Rollands asked.

"That is precisely what I am suggesting." Anneke answered.

"I was told that the story about Markus' bones being smuggled out of Jerusalem may not be true. If that is so, aren't we wasting our time?" Razier cautioned.

Anneke drew in a long and slow breath. Then she began, "We know from other sources that in fact the story that the knights tell is correct. It is my understanding that sarsens would not have cared that some old bones were taken out of the city anyway. They were not that concerned with the reverence the Venetians had for the dead. It seemed the Ottomans could care less about bones and stuff."

"Okay, you mean like the relics and all the things dear to the Catholic Church?" Razier asked.

"Well, yes I guess you might infer that. For example, The Maltese cross that Rollands is wearing. Other than the cost of the gold, they would not see much value in it." Anneke replied.

Rollands laughed as he said, "Yeah I see little value either; other than the fact that some of the knights still think I am one of them just because I wear the symbol. What they don't realize is that this whole eight points on the cross that stand for eight great virtues is drivel. For people to believe that the meek will inherit the earth or that the merciful shall obtain mercy or that the peacemakers will be blessed are the ideas of the weak and feeble minded. Have you ever seen anyone who is persecuted for their virtues inherit anything but death and humiliation?"

Razier fixed his eyes on the parchment scroll; he did not want Rollands to see his reaction. For Razier, while having different beliefs from his adversaries, in his heart was convinced that for people like Jake and Sherry, there was a certain resolve and commitment that stirred their life to action, which was very different, if not totally lacking in Rollands. For behind all the bravado and show of confidence was a man of inconsistent and incongruent behavior. This realization was a source of increasing anxiety, for Razier.

Just as the two were headed out of the door, Anneke said, "I think there is one more thing you need to know." She rolled out an old cloth about two feet by five feet. "You should observe this piece of painting taken from Guatemala back in the 1800's. This is the lost piece of Villalpando's work done in the late 1600's. If you had the original you would notice Saint Francis has burn marks on his hands and feet. These are called stigmata. Ieke you should know that Saint Francis may well have paid a very dear price for possessing the Clavicularius and the Chereb. It is said that the Stigmata never heal."

28

A NEAR HIT

The Chrysler 300 S, sped down the two lane, snake like country road, toward Castiglione. The occupants were oblivious to the threat that was just around the next curve. There at the side of the road not more than a half mile away, hidden under a pile of sticks and brush was Sal Selces, waiting patiently for their arrival. Jake and Sherry were discussing plans for the search with the Old Man.

"So what do you think the odds are that we find the Chereb at Isla Maggori?" Jake asked.

The Old Man scratched and pulled at his scraggly white beard for a moment. "Well," he said like each letter was being extracted from his mouth," if what we know of Bernardone is correct, he very well might have hidden the Chereb on the island. The thing that makes me take caution is that we are sure that the Chereb was with Pizarro in Peru in the 1500's. So how could it have been hidden on the island here after the conquests and why not in Rome; or for that matter Northern Spain or France? In any case, the island is as good a place as any to begin. Know also my young friends, Rollands will be watching and searching just as we are."

As the Old Man spoke, Sal radioed ahead that the black car had just passed his position. The long piece of nylon riddled with sixteen-penny nails was already tied to the road sign on the far side of the road. The old Toyota truck was sitting in the gravel driveway off to the side of the main road and was running. The large man was holding onto the nylon and nail rope waiting to pull it taunt. By pulling the rope the nails would be held upright just long enough to pierce the tires of the car as it passed over the hazard. At that moment the car rounded the corner and the large man pulled the nylon tight.

Too late, the driver of the Chrysler noticed the nail-ridden band just as the front tires were rolling over. By the time the car swerved and the brakes were applied, the back tires were pierced. The driver fought with the car as the air hissed out, the tires gave way to the rims of the car. Sparks flew as the sound of metal on stone filled the air. Sherry gasped as the car lurched toward the ditch. Then as suddenly as it started it was over. The car was resting with the right front tire in the ditch and the left rear wheel spinning in the air.

Dazed, just a bit by the impact, the driver yelled, "everybody out," as the Old Man had already opened the right side passenger door.

The dust was just beginning to settle as the Toyota truck rolled up and screeched to a halt. The gang descended from the truck and made a beeline for Sherry who had just staggered to a small mound of dirt not more than 15 feet from the ditched vehicle. The large thug that held the nailed rope moments earlier, was first to lunge at Sherry.

He focused his eyes on her right wrist. He saw his objective; the small band or Clavis on her wrist. As he dove at her, Sherry spun 180 degrees as she planted her heel in his groin.

He fell to the ground as three more assailants attacked. Sherry tripped over a vine and hit the ground with a thud. She felt the pain as her previously-fractured ribs stretched and strained under the pressure of the ground contact. She felt her breath leave her. Hands grabbed and scrapped at her right wrist as the Clavis was yanked off her hand. The assailant, now on all fours, scampered down the small mound of dirt.

He yelled, "Got it," as he righted himself on both feet. He began to run toward the truck.

Without warning he was upended by the blow of a tire iron. Jake with the implement in his right hand scrambled after the Clavis that was now rolling toward the ditch. Just as his fingers touched the treasure he felt the pangs of pain on his right shoulder. Guided by the rigors of technical training he cartwheeled into the ditch as he prepared to face his attacker. Now two men growled as they lunged. Jake as if it were nothing, sat in the ditch as the two flew over his head, landing on the hard pavement.

By now the roar of the truck was in his ears. In the same manner as it began it was over. The thugs climbed aboard the small truck as it turned around and almost turned over speeding away. Jake turned and ran to Sherry.

"Honey, are you alright?" He asked.

"Just peachy," she replied as she limped down the hill.

The Old Man and his driver walked up from the car as the dust settled.

"What was that all about," Jake asked as he helped Sherry down the hill.

"Well I imagine that we just received a bit of a warning from Ieke Rollands that we had better back off." The Old Man said.

"Sherry, are you okay?" The driver asked.

"I am as good as can be expected, but I think I reinjured my rib." Sherry replied.

As Sherry gasped for more air, Jake without any hesitation replied before she could speak, "I think it's in the ditch just behind the car. I had my hand on it just before the attackers lunged at me."

"It's getting dark," the Old Man said, "we had better get to looking for it."

The driver was already talking with a friend on his phone about a tow truck when the others started crawling through the ditch in the dark. The Old Man was holding the old red plastic flashlight.

After not more than two minutes Sherry said, "Look at it. It is glowing."

Less than five feet in front of her, the Clavis was actually glowing in the dark.

Sherry looked at Jake as if to say, "This is getting very strange".

Hooked to the back of the large white truck the black disabled car looked somehow older and less inviting than it did just hours before. Jake and Sherry jumped into the cab of the truck while the Old Man and the driver of the car followed behind, in the little white Fiat 500, supplied by the service repair center. After two more hours and a late evening request of the local Poliziotto to remove the bullards from the drive, the group arrived in the village of Castiglione. The owner of the Albergo La Torre was waiting at the desk as the worn-out travelers made their way inside the small white building in the center of the village.

"Do you know of a good place to eat?" Jake asked the owner.

"Let me make a call," the young dark haired woman in her early 40's said.

"Walk down one block it is on your left," she said, as she handed Jake the key to his room, number eight.

Ristorante L' Acquario was a small stone restaurant right out of the middle ages. The owner had already started the closing process prior to the group's arrival. It didn't seem to matter to him that the group showed up well after closing hours. He greeted the visitors with a wide smile as the travel weary friends sat down. Jake ordered lamb shank while the others ordered typical pasta dishes. Jake broke the ice after he had eaten half his dinner.

"Well, when can we expect the next attack?" he asked.

The Old Man said, "I think we are going to have a few days' peace now. Rollands, we can expect has been told that Sherry has the Clavis and he, Rollands, will not order another action against us until he is sure we are onto the trail of the Chereb."

Jake replied, "This is a fantastic piece of lamb and how far are we from the island?"

The Old Man laughed, "Not far at all, we will get started in the morning. I think we will be able to get a launch from the beach tomorrow."

"Alright, let's get some rest; you guys look like you were pulled through a hay bailer feet first." Sherry said.

Jake's legs felt like logs as he climbed the last few stairs to the room.

29

THE ISLAND RACE

As Kareem and Ieke walked out of the library and headed across the street in the direction of the waiting taxi, Rollands' phone rang. He pulled a black plastic case from his front pocket. Rollands stopped as Razier walked on toward the car.

"Talk to me," Rollands ordered.

The guy on the other end of the phone said, "Hey boss, this is Sal. I don't have good news for you."

"What do you mean no good news?"

"For starters I broke my arm."

"But you got the Clavis Right?"

"Well that's the other bad news. I had it but that Jake clobbered me with a tire iron and when my arm gave way I dropped the Clavis. The good news is that they may not find it either. I saw it fall into a mud hole and it was getting dark. We can check it out if you want."

"Where are you now?"

"We are at the hospital"

"We, what do you mean we?"

"Well Dujas may not make it. It seems that while he was waiting for the car to pass he ate some blackberries. It turned out they were Belladonna."

"Serves him right, what about your arm?"

"He broke both my bones; it is in a cast now."

"Get back out there, find that bracelet, track them down and let me know what they are doing. Ya got it?"

"Yes sir," Sal said.

As he caught up to Razier at the car Razier asked, "What's up?"

"We are going to have to do this ourselves; we lost a couple of guys in Italy." Rollands snapped.

"Well, where are they now?"

"They are in Perugia. Not far from where the Romans lost to Hannibal." Rollands said.

Razier quipped, "That helps a lot as he opened the rear right hand door."

"Get in, let's go," Rollands said.

The car dropped them off a few paces from the waiting plane. The fuel truck was just finishing as Rollands waived a handful of piasters at the guy filling the last tank. Razier and Rollands made a quick check of the planes exterior. In a few minutes the plane was lifting off the ground, heading as close to due north as possible. The flight from Egypt to Rome was the shortest leg of the planned trip. Razier was not clear on the next leg of the trip. In fact he had been given very few details since they were in West Africa.

"So can you update me on the current plans?" He finally managed to ask.

"Let's get this beast in the air; then, we can talk." Rollands suggested.

Within moments the plane was cruising low over the Mediterranean. They would fly in a straight line to Rome, refuel and then fly the short hop to a small strip not far from Castiglione. After the plane struggled to 8,000 feet it began to glide effortlessly. It didn't take Razier long to start the questions.

"Okay so why don't you paint in the numbers for me. I am not clear on our plan or quite frankly, why you need me at this point." Razier stated with clear frustration accenting each word.

"Hold on there chief," Rollands said, "take a few deep ones while I put this little bird on auto, then I will enlighten you."

"Please do," Razier replied.

"Here it is, plain and simple. I have spent the last ten years preparing for this. I have dreamt of the day when I, like so many great men before me, could shape and control the course of history. With the Clavicularius and the Chereb, there is nothing we can't do."

"Okay I got all that, but why not just wait for the knights to get the Chereb and then we can grab Sherry again and trade her for what you want?"

"First off, it's not all that simple. Jake, for example, was trained by the most lethal fighters there are. Think of Pizarro who conquered thousands of South American Incas with just a few hundred men. Do you really think he just walked up, grabbed the Inca and all his lieutenants and captains just gave up? No Hotshot, he had the Clavicularius and the Chereb and that is what did the job."

"Yes I heard that before. But why are these three so special?"

"Here it is as simple as I can make it for you. For some reason, don't ask me why, because it makes no difference to me, when a knight has all three the awesome power is there."

"Are you saying that you must be a knight in order for the things to work?"

"Well, let's look at the facts."

"Who was with Pizarro when he conquered the Inca?"

"Well a few other natives, a bunch of family and friends and that's about it I guess."

"Alright, you are mostly correct, but you are missing one key. Alfonso Alvarado was with him. Alfonso was a Knight of Santiago. These Knights of Santiago were special; special because Santiago was there at the beginning."

"What do you mean the beginning?"

"He was there when all this started. It's all written in the Book of Knights. In fact Santiago, it is said, wrote one of the sections."

"So what you're saying is, all you have to do is become a knight and then if you have the items you can rule the world?"

"Well Hotshot, maybe not the world but at least a big chunk of it."

The plane landed in Rome in the early afternoon. Razier noticed that Rollands was changing. For one thing he jumped out of the plane and did not bother to tie it down.

"Come on Hotshot," Rollands yelled as he headed toward a waiting taxi.

Razier tied down one wing and threw one chauk under a wheel as he jogged to Rollands and the waiting car. The car screeched as it left the airport tarmac. As they passed St. Peter's Square, Rollands jumped out of the car and motioned for Razier to join.

"See here it is." Rollands said as he pointed to a statue of St. Paul leaning on a sword. "That's the Chereb." He said.

Rollands jumped back into the vehicle and Razier followed closely behind.

"It's not far now." Rollands said as they turned the corner.

"This will do." Rollands said as he threw a few euros to the driver.

Razier scanned the Spanish steps as the two jogged past. Razier thought, *what a beautiful place,* as he took in the grandeur of the central city.

Rollands was now pushing open the door of a small castle-like building just a few steps from the large fountain.

"We're here," Rollands almost yelled.

Now inside the headquarters of the Knights of St. John in Rome, Rollands was greeted by two smallish men. Rollands introduced Razier and the older looking of the two asked Kareem to have a seat.

"I'll be back in a few," Rollands said as he followed the two men into a small office. The door closed behind them.

"Ieke," the older gentleman said, "We are concerned that you are not upholding your vows and commitment to the order."

"Where did you get that idea?" Rollands asked.

"Well we received a report from Christian Poincy in America. It said that if you showed up here that we should not be surprised to find that you have come for unethical reasons."

"Unethical reasons," Rollands said with incredulity, "I have always been committed to the order."

"Is it true that you ordered one of our own, Sherry Paul, be taken and held for ransom? Is it also true that you were behind a scheme to extract money from the United States Government?"

"You have got to be kidding. That Sherry Paul and her new husband Jake are the ones you need to be concerned about. They, as we speak, are here in Italy trying to steal the sword and other treasures from the order. Well at least one of the orders. That is why I am here. I plan to stop them in their tracks."

"So you did not take a Clavis from an underground site in South America; is that correct?"

Rollands thought for a moment then he said, "I take my vows very seriously and I would not do anything to hurt the order. You know these are dangerous times for the Cross and Order."

The younger of the two asked, "Well then you would not mind if we sent a couple of other knights with you on your mission to capture Jake and Sherry, would you?"

"Certainly not," Rollands responded. His eyes, however, betrayed a slight hesitation.

"Okay then," the older man responded, "here is what you were searching for. In the 13th century Bernardone visited the major Island on Lake Tresmone not far from Assisi. Tradition has it that he buried the instructions for the use and location of the sword. We know that Jake and Sherry are after those instructions. Your orders are to apprehend them and to bring them back to us so we might properly protect the items. As you know, these items in the wrong hands would be disastrous for the order."

"I understood that the Chereb might be in Venice and we were about to head there. Besides I like Venice much better than Umbria. But you are right; I am the only one that can counter these hypocrites Jake and Sherry. I guess I am off to Lake Tresmone. " Rollands said.

Moments later Rollands, Razier and the assigned overseers, Phaciasa and Harpises, were on the road to Perugia.

30

THE WATER WAR

The launch was waiting at the northeast end of Castiglione less than a mile from the small hotel. Jake, Sherry and the Old Man walked from the hotel down the smooth stone path, between the tiny shops and out across the park to the water. The boat was a classic wooden hull and cabin with a fifty-horse diesel engine. The pilot tipped his white cap to Sherry as the trio made their way onto the small vessel. The cabin was fitted with mahogany plank-like benches with what looked like a quarter inch of lacquer on the wood. The lake was calm and the sun was shining brightly over the distant mountain tops. As the vessel pushed off and made a turn, the largest island on the lake was immediately visible to Jake as he craned his head to look through the foggy front window. The small boat rocked to and fro as it sped toward the island. Within a few minutes the craft was securely docked on the nearly-deserted island.

Upon arrival the Old Man was greeted by a tall, slender guy with a long straight nose and penetrating brown eyes. He was dressed in a simple brown robe. After exchanging greetings and twisting bear-hugs the Old Man introduced Jake and Sherry to the slender man.

"So you are looking for a treasure here on the island." He said to Jake.

"Well, not really; we are interested in Bernardone's shrine." Jake replied.

"And so you are just on a sightseeing-tour?" the man quizzed.

A small smile was now evident on his narrow boney face. The statement belied the fact that a 'shrine' was the antithesis of what Bernardone would want, especially on the island.

"I think Old Man has told you what we are after," Jake suggested.

"Alright, let's get to it." The guide said.

He waved his hand in the direction of a small clearing now sprouting various volunteer plants and weeds adorning the top of a small hill. He shuffled along with his oversized, clown like shoes sliding on the path. The group followed as he slowly made his way up the trail toward a few small structures located on the interior of the island. After moving to the back of a small building, looking more like a shack than a permanent building, he pulled a key off the cord of his robe and slid it into the lock on the weather baked door. The door creaked open. Once inside, the smell of stale water filled the air.

Jake laughed as he said, "this smells like a pulp mill."

The mixture of humidity and dust almost made Sherry choke as she followed Jake and the Old Man down a small underground hallway. She fought back the impulse to run out. The demons of her past imprisonment in a cave still taunted her regularly.

The passage opened to a room neatly arrayed with wooden containers and clay storage jars.

"Here they are!" the slender man announced, raising his hand toward the center of the lamp lit room.

"I will leave you to your work," he announced as he shuffled back down the thin slightly-overgrown trail.

Jake looked at the Old Man and asked, "Where do we begin, there must be fifty wooden storage cases and at least twenty clay jars?"

Sherry was already using a small pry she found in a corner of the room, to open one of the cases that set on the top a column of six or so.

As she began to dig through the items, she pulled from the case a parchment piece about two feet by three feet.

She read aloud, "Significant visits from the 1800's."

She carefully placed the item back into the wooden container and replaced the lid.

"Okay," she said, "I think we will find what we are looking for toward the bottom of the stack. If my hunch is correct the things we are looking for are going to be at the bottom of the pile."

"How do you know that?" Jake questioned with a puzzled look on his face.

"It is clear that these are piled in a pretty solid chronology." Sherry responded.

Jake and the Old Man began unloading the containers until they located the one on the brown clay filled dirt floor.

The top creaked as the last few nails released their grip on the wood. She wrangled the top off and like the first container; the second yielded a parchment sheet.

She again began to read, "Chronology of visits of Bernardone to the island."

She dug half-way down the inside of the container and pulled out another brittle page.

She read slowly:

> "A Divine spark, the Chereb waits. The faithful still and humbly seek, where bats sleep and bells ring the Clarian's call. He the Greater, Santiago will protect. Paulo, Anatolia, Pierre Auvergne, James and back, treasures certain to suffer to raise; pompous power and pointless greed, to dust."

"This is it!" the Old Man said, "We need search no further, it is not here."

"What do you mean?" Jake asked.

"The words Sherry read are all we need to know. They tell us what Bernardone did with the Chereb."

Sherry looked down at the Clavis on her wrist as she felt a slight twinge, like a static shock. She thought she saw a small puff of white smoke escape from the bracelet. She felt a shudder run up her spine.

"Let's get going. I don't like what I am feeling right now. I think that bad things may happen," She said.

She and the others rushed toward the door of the crumbling structure.

"What is going on with you?" Jake asked as he jogged to catch up.

"Jake, it was like I just saw a ghost or something. I think Ariel is telling us to get out of here."

"Ariel?" Jake asked. "I haven't heard you speak of Ariel in a long while."

The group was now moving down the small stone-filled path at a trot. The Old Man was following from behind as they made their way back to the waiting launch. The captain didn't have time to put out the ramp as Sherry, Jake and the Old Man jumped on board.

"Let's go!" Jake yelled at the captain.

The engine rumbled as it turned over. The little vessel began to back away from the deteriorating dock. As the captain slid the small black-knobbed shift handle forward, the boat surged. As the launch began to cruise, a much larger craft was closing rapidly on the rig. A sense of anxiety began to well up in Jake, as he now saw more clearly what Sherry sensed back at the shed. The other vessel was coming at them at full speed. She was sensing the approach of others.

Jake demanded of the captain, "Can you get this thing to move any faster?"

He noticed the captain's hand as it pressed the throttle forward as far as it could go. The noise coming from the inboard engine overshadowed any other sound as the captain fixed his eyes on the gauges. The other boat was now turning and pursuing from about a quarter mile behind.

The Old Man said, "Everyone calm down. Castiglione is less than a half mile away. "

Jake looked over at Sherry who sat on the port side, staring at the approaching boat. She was somber yet showed no sign of fear.

Jake scampered over as the boat lurched sideways. He crashed into Sherry as he made his way to the plank next to her. She did not flinch.

"What do you see?" He asked.

Sherry yelled in his ear, "I think I see Ieke, Razier and five or six others in that boat."

As the approaching craft came close, Jake could see Ieke and the others. Clearly the other vessel was faster and was now only 40 or 50 yards from the launch they rode. He could see the captain of the other boat motioning to cut the engine.

Jake scampered back to the captain, like a drunken sailor and said, "Keep going; let's get to shore."

The captain nodded in agreement. Just as the vessel was making its final turn toward the beach, the other boat lunged in the direction of the launch. The wash of the wake nearly swamped the smaller craft as the captain pulled back on the throttle. As the small boat came to a stop, the large boat turned a wide circle and headed right at Jake's boat. As the larger craft was less than 10 feet away Jake and Sherry dove over board. Sherry clutched the scroll in her left hand as she felt the cold water rush over her head. Jake looked back, as he saw the small boat he had just left go airborne.

He dove under water as he watched the larger boat come to rest just inches above his head. He looked back and the prop was turning in slow motion. Then it stopped spinning altogether. His lungs were beginning to burn as they called for more oxygen. When he slid to the back of the boat and raised his head, he noticed a large hole in the side of the bottom. As he swam toward shore, he saw Sherry to his right and 20 feet in front. She was now walking on the bottom. He stopped swimming and noticed that he was now in less than four feet of water. He followed Sherry as she made her way toward shore. He did not see the Old Man or the captain. He did see a commotion in the water not more than 50 feet behind him.

31

QUESTIONS AND ANSWERS

As Jake stepped onto the shore, Sherry was already marching up the hill toward the road one-hundred feet ahead of him. As he strode to the gravel road, Jake turned back to see the Old Man and the captain of the boat he had just been in still hanging on to the now slightly-submerged vessel.

The other craft was bobbing on the water with smoke billowing from the rear engine compartment. Jake watched Ieke waving his hands at a vessel that was moving in that direction. Jake turned back after what was a momentary hesitation and started running toward Sherry. He caught her as she was starting up an old stone stairway. They had used the same route just a few hours earlier on their approach to the boat that morning. As the two made their way up the uneven stairs, a throng of onlookers were headed down from the castle toward the stranded boats.

Jake thought, *we can blend into the crowd and Ieke and his gang will not be able to track our location. I hope Old Man and the captain will be alright.*

Sherry said, "I think we can head back to the hotel without anyone seeing us if we move fast."

Jake nodded his head as the two vanished from sight, behind the walls of the old castle. As they walked along, Jake noticed Sherry still carried the now water-soaked parchment. When they made their way inside the hotel the owner was standing at the desk.

Jake stopped and asked, "Has anyone asked our whereabouts in the last few hours?"

She replied, "I haven't heard or seen anyone that is interested in you guys or the Old Man."

Jake said, "If anyone inquiries, please don't let them know we are here."

He and Sherry made their way to the small room and bolted the door.

The driver of the small launch approached the two men clinging to the half-submerged water craft and extended an oar. The Old Man grabbed onto the blade and pulled the sinking boat to the stern of the rescuer's launch. The captain and the Old Man climbed aboard and helped to fasten the line to the rear of the rescue craft.

As the boat slowly motored toward the shore, the Old Man heard Ieke Rollands yell, "This is not over; I am coming after you."

Once safely on the beach, the Old Man assisted the captain in securing the craft to the shore as the rescue craft made its way to the other now half-submerged, stranded boat.

With sadness on his face, the Old Man walked slowly up the same rock steps Jake and Sherry had just traversed as more people gathered on the shore watching as the other craft, with its badly damaged hull; slowly made its way to shore.

The Old Man moving stiff legs like a worn-out robot made his way up the steps of the hotel. Reaching the landing and let out a slow sigh as he knocked on Jake and Sherry's door.

Once inside and after a laughing spell that lasted what seemed like forever, Jake, Sherry and the Old Man began to discuss the strange poem. It now was even more damaged by the workings of time and the effects of water on the soaked hide.

"You do know that Santiago is James the Greater don't you?" The Old Man suggested.

"So you said you know where the Chereb is." Jake responded.

"Well I have my opinion," the Old Man replied.

"You're Opinion?" Jake asked as more of a command.

"Here's what I know," the Old Man began. "We can assume that Bernardone wrote this, can't we?"

"I think we can." Sherry interjected.

"Let's assume that what the knights have told us about Bernardone is true. We know for example that after he returned from Egypt he founded the order of sisters called the Poor Clares."

"Okay I'm with you on that." Jake commented.

"So where do we know that he visited after returning with the Items?" The Old Man asked.

Jake asked, "Returning what items?"

Sherry, now standing, replied, "I get it now; it all fits. Bernardone visited Galicia of the West, which, if am not mistaken, is part of what is now Spain or Portugal. It is said that James, was a friend or maybe even the brother of the Maestro but I don't think so. He went to Galicia where a temple was built under his name, which in Spanish is called Santiago. He had the Chereb."

Jake said, "That makes sense. Bernardone founded the Poor Clares in 1224. I bet the Chereb is in the bell tower of that Franciscan convent. The poem we discovered on the island was kind of like a Last Will and Testament. He penned it, making it his desire to ensure the Chereb was to be housed there. "

"I guess we are off to Galicia, Spain." Sherry said.

"Just a minute," Jake replied. "I think we learned in Lima that one of the Knights of Santiago had the Chereb and wore the Cuffs on his wrists when Pizarro conquered the Inca. So why do we want to make the same mistake that the Spaniards made. By removing the Chereb and by combining it with the Clavicularius are we not making a big blunder?"

Sherry replied, "I learned from a fine person that it is not whether or not one possesses the items; it is the ends to which the items are directed. That is, whether used for good or ill determines the fate of the possessor."

Jake looked at Sherry and shook his head as if to say, "Where did she come up with this?"

"Well, I guess you may be correct." The Old Man said. "Remember that after the victory over the Inca, things unraveled for Alvarado and the Knights of Santiago. He eventually lost everything for which he fought. The desire for power overwhelmed the desire to do good— that's when things turned south so to speak. That is why I remind you that this is a very serious undertaking. As I tell you again today, Ieke Rollands and those like him will do almost anything to get their hands on the power and fortune that these items represent. You are correct that the Chereb was returned to Spain after Alvarado ended his life in ruins."

Jake reasoned, "Actually, it makes a lot of sense; since we know that Pierre De Montaigu was a Gaul. While he came from France because of the distances and lack of accurate communications, he may not have known that Bernardone would take the Chereb to Spain, one thing is clear he trusted Bernardone. Bernardone or the Sultan gave the Chereb to Spain. That very well would be why Bernardone penned the poem we now possess. Anyway, we don't have a better theory, do we?"

"I guess not." Sherry replied.

"So what are we waiting for?" Jake asked.

32

UNDER THE TOWER

The Old Man, Sherry and Jake threw their belongings into suitcases with a flurry of activity. The vibration of slamming doors sent shockwaves throughout the small lodge. The car and driver wheeled up to the front door of the small lodge as Jake and the Old Man dropped bags into the opened trunk. Sherry was already in the car as Jake and the Old Man slid into the car. Within a few minutes, they were driving down the highway toward Milan. It took less than two hours for the trio to reach the train station in Milan. Moving out of the car, the three strode with urgency in their gait. The driver watched as the three ran into the train station waiting area. Less than thirty minutes later they boarded the train for Compostela De Santiago.

A few hours earlier, back at the lake, Ieke Rollands and the others were pulled from the water. They caught another launch and made their way to land. Ieke cornered the guide that kept Bernardone's 'monument' and the surrounding structures secure. He was not in the mood for politeness. He raised his voice in anger and asked where Jake and the others had been searching. The keeper guide hesitated. Ieke lashed out and beat the man with the back of his fist. After numerous strikes across the face, the slender monk in his own humble way submitted to the demand and tottered toward the stores where Jake and the others discovered the poem. Once inside the small structure, Ieke wasted no time. First he secured the monk with a small piece of hemp he found coiled in the corner. Once the monk was securely tied, Ieke began making his requirements known.

"What were they after," Ieke demanded.

"I already told you I don't know," the guide said, as he worked at the ropes tied around his hands.

"I know you know; let's just make this easy on all of us." Ieke scowled just inches from the guide's nose.

As he turned his eyes skyward the monk said, "As I told you, they were interested in the documents written by Bernardone."

"Okay now we are getting somewhere. And where are these writings?"

"They are here in one of these boxes." The guide said.

Ieke glanced over at the stacks of boxes with a frown on his face.

"Which one?" Ieke demanded.

"I am not sure; I left them alone up here. There are hundreds of sheets in each chest."

Ieke backhanded the guide across the right side of his face. The guide flinched as a trace of blood flowed in an erratic pattern from the corner of his mouth.

As the two knights reached out to stop Rolland's tantrum, they were repulsed by a vortex, some kind of force surrounding Ieke. They seemed spellbound by his evil power.

"Tell us all what you know of this Bernardone." Ieke yelled.

"All I know is that he possessed great power and that he spent time on this island resting and writing. Some of these chests contain many of his writings. Others just contain maps and mementos. It is rumored that Bernardone came back here from his visit to Egypt with even greater power. After he returned from that trip, he received the stigmata."

"And what are the stigmata," Ieke asked.

"Well you know the so called marks of the Master. They are like wounds on the feet and hands or they are symbolic of suffering or something like that. It is said he carried them with him to the grave. Uh, anyway, it is also said that he brought back a small dagger like sword that had mystical powers. Now it is said that he buried it here. No one knows for sure."

"So that is what Jake and Sherry were after," Ieke stated.

"Well I don't know, but it seems that they were more interested in his writings."

With that Ieke ordered Razier and the others to search, "every fricken' inch of this dung hole."

"He grabbed the guide by the shirt sleeves and tossed him out of the shack. The monk hit the ground with a thud. Ieke then focused his anger on the stacks of neatly stored chests. He began throwing the chests out the door as the guide looked on with disgust and disbelief in his eyes.

Razier walked around the entire inside of the shed looking for any sign of trap doors or hidden storage areas. The other knights followed Ieke's lead and began tossing the chests out the door as Rollands ordered. They joined, not out of respect for Rollands, but because they were loyal to the code of the knights. Their leader seemed deranged. Yet he was still powerful in persuasion. Rollands, with speed and aplomb, sifted through the documents strewn around the path.

After nearly two hours, Rollands said, "There is nothing we need here; let's get back to Castiglione."

As he walked by the chest that contained the poem that Jake and Sherry found he paused.

"Wait a minute," he said.

He grabbed his wrist as it was paining him. Razier noticed a grimace on Ieke's face. He stooped down and fixed his gaze on the parchment attached to the top.

The parchment contained a complete inventory of the documents housed in the chest. By now the guide was sitting on the side of the path. Shock and fear were still in his eyes. Ieke looked over at him, looked back at the chest and ran his finger down the list. His index finger paused at item L.22.38.

"Where is it, find L.22.38?"

He ordered, "Find document L.22.38."

The group pored over the strewn documents. They continued for an hour more and found no document. Ieke turned to the guide and asked, "What does document L.22.38 say?"

The guide responded, "It was a poem that talks about bell towers, and Santiago and some things like that."

Ieke walked in a straight line to the guide, grabbed him by the neck and accentuating each word said, "What does it M E A N."

"The guide, with tremulous in his voice said, "I, I think it might have something to do with Santiago de Compostela."

With that Ieke let loose of the guide and headed down the path motioning in the direction of the launch with his hand.

Meanwhile Jake, Sherry and the Old Man boarded the train headed toward Santiago de Compostela. The semi-private car was the only reasonable accommodation left. The group ended up sharing the car with a young man who was escaping the poverty and oppression of Romania. Jake and the young man discussed politics in the United States and in Romania. He was quite taken with Jake and Sherry and gave Sherry a beautiful hand-embroidered table runner made by his grandmother in Romania. He told Jake that he was escaping to Spain. He related to Jake that he was shot in the back and then imprisoned in Romania as a teen for drawing Mickey Mouse ears on a political poster of Crachenco, the Romanian strongman, who had the young man's father, a University professor, and his uncle murdered for insurrection. "Would you like to come to dinner with us?" Sherry inquired of the young fellow.

"How kind," he replied as he smiled at Sherry.

At dinner he shared, "I and a group of friends are headed to freedom in Spain. There, we have a friend that is waiting for us. We will help him with a small apartment building project. See here; we all have fake passports and we are going to join our friend in Compostela."

He provided for Jake a detailed map of the Cathedral and even the location of Santiago's grave site. Early in the morning as the train crossed the Spanish border, members of the Spanish police knocked at the door of the car. Then they broke into the car and hauled the young man from the sleeper, as they did to his friends in other cars. Sherry looked over at the Old Man as a tear made its way to his lower jaw. As the train pulled out of the station the last sight Jake recalled was the young man and the others in a line at the station under police guard. Jake clutched the hand-written map and Sherry pressed her index finger on the table runner caressing it with the sensitivity of a new mother as they made their way toward Galicia. With sadness in their hearts they arrived at the Cathedral De Santiago De Compostela.

"I understand there is nothing we can do to save the young Romanian. But I am so sad." Sherry said.

"This is the essence of love; knowing that you cannot control the life and decisions of others. We can be there if there is good to do. If not, we mourn for their loss." The Old Man shuddered.

Sherry looked at Jake and Said, "It breaks my heart; there is so much pain and suffering on this earth."

Jake nodded his head in a slow and deliberate fashion.

The old Romanesque church adorned with the opulence of the 19th century somehow, to Sherry, seemed out of place.

Bernardone would not have hidden the Chereb here, Jake thought as they approached the massive structure with its many spires. While the beauty of the facade was humbling, it also seemed wrong somehow. To imagine that the church existed on that site for over a thousand years added to the paradoxical nature of the experience. A young man was apprehended and sent back to a cruel and demeaning existence because of his only crime, which was to want freedom and a better life. While a few thousand miles away people were free to blossom and prosper. Jake was the first to put words to thoughts.

"I don't think we are in the right place. This couldn't be the location; it is too opulent." He said.

As they paused to take in the grandeur of the Church, the Old Man's face was tense, like he was in great pain. Jake could not help but notice. The Old Man replied as if he were reciting:

> "Keep in mind my son; the religious institutions have always suffered from the excesses of men. There have always been tyrants and without a seismic change in spirit there always will be. That is why we must fight for the good.

Did you know that the bells in the tower and the massive gates of the Cathedral were taken by the Moors and mounted on the Cordoban Mosque during the conquest? They and many of the relics were removed and then taken by Christian warriors and put in France after recapturing the region. Such was the history of the Cross, the Crescent and the Star."

A tear ran down his cheek as he finished his words.

He paused, cleared his throat and then continued:

"Isn't it possible that Bernardone knew and understood that men of power see little value in the common man and want to surround themselves with treasures of their conquests? Think back to Pizarro and the other conquistadores. They led men to the new world on 'Holy' missions. In reality, they were contaminated by their own thirsts for gold and riches.

Do you think that the Maestro or Bernardone, for that matter, would have approved? Most assuredly they would not. Yet, while the evil is evident, think of our own plight. Where is it, on this vast planet that those who are driven by a lust for power and wealth also want to do good? Does not the Maestro teach us to respect those in power? He cared for the poor. Bernardone befriended the Sultan and he honored the Grand Master and the Pope. He was driven to this even when the Sultan and the Grand Master were at war.

He used those in power to bring assistance to the poor and suffering. As we walk forward my young friends, you must be committed to doing the same. Are you ready to bring good and to let the Maestro handle your enemies?

Jake thought for a moment and then replied, "I appreciate your guidance. When we keep our eyes fixed on the path the

Maestro laid out, then we find our way, no matter what our past; heathen, Jew, Christian, Muslim, Buddhist, or the misguided leader, of whatever religious group."

Sherry suggested, "Let's go see the Sisters; they will know all the secrets of this place. I am sure they will trust our motives. After all, you will be with us Old Man."

Moments later the three were in a small unpretentious room. They spoke with a small group of sisters of the order of the Poor Clares a group that Bernardone help to found.

One of the sisters began to provide a history for the group.

"Keep in mind that there have been spiritual journeys going on here since the middle ages and it is said that this site was a place of Christian worship since the beginning. Did you know that this site is third only to Jerusalem and Rome as a pilgrim site?"

Sherry said, "Well actually we were briefed on this but we, as you know, are looking for a specific artifact. We are confident you can help us. It is our understanding that when the Moors raided the site in the conquest, they did not disturb the relics in Santiago's tomb, is that correct?"

"You are on target, but are you also aware that Knights of Santiago also were participants in the conquests in the Americas. So why do you think what you search for is here?"

"Well, for one thing we have been to Lima and other parts of South America and we have reason to believe that the Chereb was returned here after the unfortunate death of Alfonso Alvarado." the Old man stated with authority.

Upon hearing the Old Man speak she did not hesitate, "Let us have a look," the Reverend Mother said.

Sherry, surgeon like and with the utmost care unrolled the scroll on the desk. As Jake scanned the faces, it was clear that the sisters gathered in the room were shocked. After what seemed like silent eternity, the Reverend Mother finally spoke.

"Okay we are convinced that your mission is just. We will show you what we know, but be informed, we have to tell the leaders in Rome of your mission."

The Old Man replied, "We understand your requirements."

The sister led the group out of the area. The party went down a back hall, through an old wooden set of doors and down a small spiral staircase. Now deep in the bowls of the building they found themselves in a small dark and cave like room.

"I must inform you that we cannot be in the area when you do your search because Bernardone and others have given a solemn warning that danger awaits those that are not sanctioned and those who do not possess the Clavis. The faithful are ones to be granted permission to be in the presence of the Chereb. If you would excuse us, we will leave you now."

As she finished her last word she and the other sisters left the room. Jake noticed that the room seemed to become brighter and strangely more still as Sherry approached a stone cased box, two feet long and about 18 inches wide. It was no deeper than six inches. Jake and the Old Man knelt down and bowed their heads over the stone box.

The Old Man said, "As we undertake this effort, let us be reminded that this is a task not of this world but one of heavenly initiations. We approach this undertaking with humility and thanksgiving."

Jake Replied, "I agree."

The Old Man bent slowly toward the container. As he did his hair and beard flowed out touching the top. Jake approached from the other side. The box was closed. The exterior was protected by a very hard and extremely dense wood. The top was fastened with long iron pins. Jake removed each fastener with long handled pincers Sherry handed to him. A large medal lock still remained and connected the wooden top to the box. After the pins were removed, the top had to be pried off.

Jake asked, "What now?"

Sherry placed her wrist directly against the surface of the lock. The Clavis she wore made contact with the rusted steel hinge. Jake saw a blue light similar to that of a welding torch flame. He heard a popping and snapping sound. As the sound occurred the hinge released its hold on the box. After the lock was unhinged and the pins were removed, the top had to be pried off.

As Jake and the Old Man began to lift, a whirling wind began to fill the room. Slowly at first, then as the cover slid off the top, the lowly hiss turned to a roar. As the lid was lifted, Jake saw the white hair of the Old Man begin to change form.

What was once a scraggly white beard flowing from a crop of long white hair began to take on life-like characteristics? Without warning the room began to shine and the sound of distant thunder was heard. A white pigeon-like bird fluttered up from the old man's face and landed on Sherry's shoulder. It seemed to come out and away from the beard. Sherry moved forward and raised her right hand out over the container. It was the hand that the Clavis was on. Suddenly, the Clavis glowed with a bright green and purple haze. She stooped over and the bird seemed to transform into a small dagger like sword not more than a foot long.

As she touched the Chereb, she felt heat in her right hand and she was inclined to raise the Chereb over her head. She resisted as she was now focused on Jake and the Old Man as they fell to their knees and inclined their heads.

33

THE INTERCEPTED MESSAGE

As the plane started its final descent into JFK airport the two women continued their discussion. Ann was weaving an even- more-detailed story from her expert knowledge and skilled reporting ability. Ruth was entranced and totally unaware of the passage of time.

"Okay so how did Rollands catch up with Jake and Sherry, or didn't he?" Ruth asked.

"Well you are getting a little ahead of me," Ann said. "You see, it is very important that you understand what was going on in Raziers head as he continued to follow Rollands in Italy.

"Ieke and Razier were sitting at a table outside a small café in Oriento, Italy. The wind was causing the canvas of the table umbrella to flap at a slow but steady beat. It was uncharacteristic for this time of year. The mood was somber and Ieke was more cantankerous than usual. Razier was moving fast as he leafed through a copy of a small pamphlet he picked up on the path to the island shack they tore up just a few days earlier. It reviewed the life of Saint Francis. He did not say a word the entire breakfast. He just read through the material."

"Did he think it strange that a man of wealth and privilege would give up everything in order to serve the poor and to work for peace?" Ruth asked.

"Well, I can tell you that Razier spent most of his life in pursuit of what he thought was good. It boiled down to living two lives. The first, working with and teaching American kids the meaning of symbols and the power of numbers. And the second, a hidden life, in the support of the jihad. While he spent much of his time in espionage, he had also been responsible for the brutal and cowardly kidnapping of Sherry Paul. So he was in a way— searching."

"How did you discover that…?" Ruth asked.

The stewardess interrupted the conversation. She reminded them to straighten their seat backs and faster their seat belts.

"Well, as I said, Razier spoke in great detail to Clay, our reporter and he confirmed much of what I told you. Anyhow, this and other things he had done were beginning to weigh him down. As he read and reviewed the accounts of Bernardone's life, he couldn't help but make a comparison between what he had chosen and that which he was reading of, Francisco Bernardone.

"On the other hand, seated just across the table from Razier, Ieke was almost in a frenzy. He talked in detail of the Chereb. Rollands was beginning to make a habit of chanting, 'I have to have it before they do, Jake and Sherry can't own it. It is mine.'"Ann said.

"Frenzy, that's weird. What was he doing?" Ruth asked.

"He got up from the table and made repeated phone calls, speaking with his small underground army of disenfranchised young men and women and in some cases well-connected wealthy and powerful people. They were supporters who had given up any inclination of making this world a better place for all. They wanted power and the more the better.

"As Razier listened to and reflected on the conversations, he identified a set of themes. Ieke exhorted them to satisfy their own greedy self-interests, money and more power. He reminded them that they deserved reward and these payoffs were coming to them soon. Razier watched Ieke and listened as Rollands schemed and ferreted. Razier was well aware of the rewards that Rollands promised. Simply put, Razier, in the end, could be at the right hand of one of the most powerful and most evil people on the planet. But near the end Razier could not help but wonder whether or not this was the best way to find God's will.

"Without warning he broke his silence, 'I have been wondering just how you are going to accomplish your goals when we get the Chereb?' Razier asked."

"With eyes flaming in anger Rollands replied, 'Are you that thick headed? Don't you understand, when we get the Chereb there is nothing that can stop us. With all the unrest in Syria and the African states and with the diverse factions vying for power, we will have it all. I will be able to control much of the oil and power in the world. And who do you suppose would be my right hand man? Do you think I can trust these Europeans or these hot headed Camel jockeys? Come on Hotshot, you and I will run the whole thing. We will be unstoppable.'"

"Razier looked and listened finding it hard to follow logic of the rant. It was a new version of the sermon he had heard so many times before. Deep in his heart he was becoming convinced that the path they were walking would only end with more death and more destruction. Rollands stood for everything he had learned was wrong— everything that was not on the path to Mecca. Razier was convinced that Rolland's god has two major attributes, power and money. This was not what the mission was supposed to be about. Razier saw the evil of the man and the fallacy of the man's message."

"So what happened," Ruth asked.

"As Razier thought about these things he heard the buzz of Rollands' phone. As Rollands walked into the adjoining hallway, he heard him say, 'No we have no guns, can you imagine the difficulties they might bring to us crossing the border? Besides, Sherry still has the information we need. She never gave it up even in the cave. That's great we will be on the next flight.'"

"So did Razier know who Rollands was speaking to?" Ruth asked

"Well not really," Ann said, "he was smart enough to know that a lot of difficult and ugly action was planned. He recalled Rollands saying 'Okay Hotshot, we are on our way to Spain. It seems that Jack and Jill are in Galicia. We had better hurry I think they have our sword!'"

"'How do you know?' Razier asked."

"'Well I just got a call from a friend in Rome. He said he spoke with one of the nuns at a Cathedral in Composada de Santiago.'"

34

POWER OF LIGHT

The Old Man walked over to a small slatted bench at the far end of the room. As was his usual pattern he dropped to his knees. He placed his hands on the slats. He bowed his head slowly and closed his eyes. He did not move for nearly five minutes. He lifted his head and he struggled his way to his feet, it was clear that he had less flexibility and strength than he once had. Jake, having climbed to his feet, saw the grimace on the Old Man's face as he was now standing erect. The Old man seemed to be tired but there was more. He showed the signs of pain that comes less from physical stress than from the ravages of internal, deep in the heart, trauma. For just a moment Jake thought about how fleeting life was. Jake wondered how long it would be before his own body would begin to show the ravages of time. Jake turned his head toward the Old Man as the Old Man began to speak.

"Jake and Sherry, you are now in possession of the most important and powerful force known to man. You will be tested to the end of your strength and challenged more than you have ever been challenged before. That is one thing I can assure you. If there is any doubt about the correctness of your mission or value of these possessions— it would be better for you to walk away now before it is too late for all of us."

Jake turned his face to Sherry and noticed that she was glowing as if the sun had somehow penetrated the dark stone walls and was highlighting only her. She was smiling the broadest deepest smile he had ever seen. Jake now fixed his eyes on the Old Man.

"I for one am committed to our mission and there is nothing that can deter me." Jake said as loud as he dared.

"But do you really know what the mission is?" The Old Man scolded.

"Well," Jake said emphasizing each letter, "we are to prevent Rollands from getting the Chereb. That's easy but what we do in the future is the difficult part."

"Getting the gift was always the easy part. Caring for it has been the challenge. We are going to find that caring for this gift is the greatest effort yet." Sherry added.

Jake looked over at Sherry. He saw that she was glowing like the brightest star on the clearest night. Her face was almost translucent and her eyes were inviting and yet sad. Jake wondered what she meant by 'the challenge'.

Sherry turned to the Old Man and asked, "Do you mind if I spend a little time with Jake. We have a lot to discuss."

The Old Man stood and with shoulders slumped forward and head down, walked out.

35

PREPARING FOR BATTLE

The captain lifted the microphone and informed the passengers that he had been given final authority to land. Ruth and Ann paid little attention as they continued to discuss Rollands and his plans to get his hands on the Chereb.

Ruth asked, "So I understand that Ieke was frantic. But why was he so driven to harm Sherry and Jake?"

Ann Replied, "Ieke was now in a fully aggressive mode. He was pulling together a small team of killers. He knew that in order to secure the Chereb and the other Clavis he must bring enough stealthy fighters to surprise and overwhelm Jake, Sherry and the others. He lost valuable time and he had limited capacity to know where the prizes were and when they would be moved. He was in a weakened position in large part due to lost time but also because many now saw him for what he was. He had alienated those who had been his friends and supporters. He was now bringing unprincipled people from the seedier side of the business, in order to accomplish his purpose."

"Was that his major weakness?" Ruth asked.

"Well, his major weakness was that he used many who knew him when he built some of the most successful campaigns against near eastern forces during the 1990s. He had burned almost all his bridges by then. He was abandoned by the most highly placed knights and most of the military leaders in the American and European clandestine services. He had been motivated by selfish desire and not from a joy in service to others." Ann said.

"Can you really know someone's motives?" Ruth asked.

"He knew that his time had run out. In his psychotic and deranged condition, he had been abandoned by most who were solid and loyal souls with fair-minded ideals. If he did not enhance his power within the knights he once resisted, he would be reduced to a common thug. One thing he had not lost was the power to control the weak-minded with his words." Ann replied.

"So what was going on with Razier at that time?" Ruth quizzed.

"Razier for his part knew that Ieke, his mentor and ticket to creditability as well as responsibility was on the wrong track. He saw firsthand that Ieke said he wanted to improve the world while his actions were brash, harsh, and filled with a drive to make him greater while he used and often destroyed all those who had been the most loyal. Many of these followers wanted to serve the needy you know, those being abused by the rich and powerful. While Razier felt sorry for Carlos Castilano whom Ieke abandoned to rot in jail. Razier knew that Ieke and Carlos where both pride filled beings. They seemed not to care for the poor and needy." Ann said.

"Why did Razier stick with Ieke so long?" Ruth asked.

"Razier now knew that to support Ieke was to oppose Allah and to expand greed and arrogance. He believed that Ieke still trusted and valued the service He provided. The Clavis Ieke wore on his left hand troubled Razier. It was like he was getting a code or signal to alter direction. Yet until recently, he was too busy to listen.

"These messages were not in words, they were in a sense magnetic, in some cases they pushed him and in others they pulled. Still what really gnawed deep in his heart was that he was not doing what these impulses were telling him to do. He was in conflict."

"So where were they when all this was going on?" Ruth wondered.

36

THE FUTURE REVEALED

Sherry sat down next to Jake and turned her head so that her eyes were only inches from his.

"Jake you and I have been blessed to find a real purpose in our lives. Now let me take this last chance to remind you that we are, even as I speak, in grave danger. There is nothing you or I can do about it. We are here and we have been given a wonderful gift. This gift is only given to us because of our commitment to the Maestro. Like Bernardone before us, we have a chance to shine the light on the dark side of the earth. I have been a friend to you as you have been to me. Now is our time. I know that I will not be with you much longer. You will be asked to go forward alone in a strange and difficult adventure."

"What? What are you saying?" Jake asked.

"I am saying that the end of our mission is near and I will not be as available to guide you. You will have to go forward with your own strength and skills. You will not see Old Man; he will seem to be assessable you. You must do the right thing; without fear or concern for your own well-being."

"What is going to happen?" Jake inquired.

"You know that shortly Ieke will find us and he will not stop until he has what he desires. He desires the Chereb and the Clavis. He will do what he must." Sherry said.

Sherry pulled Jake to her chest and held him tightly. Slowly she pulled her head back and she kissed Jake with all the passion she could muster. Jake felt the press of her lips and beating of her heart and he began to be at peace.

"We can get this done I am sure of it. But you are acting like it is the end and that does not feel good." Jake stated.

Slowly Sherry slid her hands across Jake's shoulders while Jake kept his gaze fixed on her sparkling eyes. He felt them pulling him closer, while at the same time filling him with fear. Sherry slowly moved over and placed the Chereb in her waistband. Jake noticed the light in the room turned to low glow.

Sherry walked out of the room as Jake followed.

As they walked down the large stone steps, the Old Man was waiting in the black Chrysler below. As Jake looked into his face, he noticed a strange, almost eerie countenance. The Old man was streaming pain from his eyes and his entire being reflected it. Jake opened the rear door as Sherry slid in ahead of him.

After the door locks latched the Old Man said, "We are off to the USA, Christian has asked us to return ASAP. He has reason to believe that Ieke and some renegades are on their way to intercept us. Someone in Rome tipped him off that we were in Galicia. I have booked a room for this evening and by tomorrow we are on our way to DC."

A short time later the car pulled up on the square of the old town in Galicia. Across the park the traveling vendors were closing their small cargo vans at the end of the day. As Sherry got out of the car she noticed a small girl sobbing as she sat in the grass a few steps away. Sherry walked over and knelt next to the little thing.

"Are you Okay," Sherry inquired in perfect Spanish.

As the little girl looked into Sherry's warm and accepting eyes her continence changed. She began to smile. Sherry touched her on the shoulder.

"We had a bad day. We did not sell one thing," the little girl said.

"Well tomorrow will be brighter for you, just you wait and see. " Sherry said.

"I like you! "The little girl yelled as she started back toward the white van and her beckoning mother.

Sherry walked back toward the grand hotel as Jake watched and waited just outside the grand old hotel entrance.

37

CHASE IS ON

Ieke and Razier were sitting in a large abandoned farm in central Italy. There were nearly thirty individuals who had been called from The United States, Europe and beyond sitting with them.

Ieke began, "You now know why we are gathered here together. We have seen our countries torn apart by those who oppose us. There are those who say they are out to free people and to bring goodness to the world, but that is not what they do. These people have been systematically derailing all the good things we want to do. We have struck out against these people and tried to counter their evil acts. We must extinguish this cancer from the world once and for all. The one thing we know must be done, we have to cut out this cancer and take what is ours. Our next step is to capture this Sherry Paul, and to cut down the child-like Jake Rader and the others who follow the burned out Old Man. This old white haired Indian that hangs out with them is the source of their weakness and he must be eliminated; a prize for the one who brings his head on a platter. I have chosen you because you want to be great and you know that I would make you great. You want to support me because you know that you would be part of the great establishment we are creating together.

"When we capture them and take those things that are ours we will begin to put life back on the right path. We will hunt them down and destroy them. Then we will set up the most powerful and wonderful organization on this sick planet." Ieke told Razier.

He walked over to a large desk and fingered a standard sheet of paper. He looked down at the document as he began to slowly wander through the group.

"Now as you know Sherry Paul or whatever she now calls herself, must be brought to justice. She is cunning and evil. You must know that she will not be easy to eliminate. Remember she still has many knights in her corner and some are the most dangerous. With that warning I send you out with one simple task. Neutralize her and bring me the Chereb and the Clavis. Each of you was provided the most up to date information as to where this group is and what you are up against. I am here to support you and know that you would be successful in your mission." Rollands said.

With that Ieke walked out. The meeting was concluded and the stage was set for a major showdown."

Razier was sitting in his sleeper chair as the TGV train sped through the French countryside at over 200 Km per hour. The chair was reclined and his eyes were closed. He was thinking about his role in the operation, as Ieke and the three others laughed obnoxiously in the background. Razier had been with Ieke for years and he was reflecting on the many experiences they had undertaken. With a slight smile, he recollected the meetings he first had with Ieke. Carlos introduced him via a letter.

The letter merely said: "You would love this guy; he is so irreverent and sophisticated."

Razier admitted to himself that Ieke was at least that, especially irreverent? He remembered that the letter invited him to a meeting in downtown Renton, Washington at the Old Melrose Grill. Ieke ordered salmon. It wasn't pen raised but very fresh wild caught while Razier ate prime rib.

Ieke asked Razier if he wanted to, "do a little mischief in support of the jihad."

That was the beginning of the long road of lies and destruction that Ieke led him down over nearly a decade. Now Razier was persona non grata and Ieke had shown himself not to be a savior but a hoax.

"How did this happen?" Razier mumbled to himself as he shook his head in disbelief.

Ieke and the others continued their mindless chatter as the night closed in on the train. In just a few short hours they would be in Galicia Spain. Ieke brandished the Clavis as he sarcastically ridiculed the robe of Mustafa, his body guard.

Rollands laughed, "You look like an old goat herder."

It was nearly 3:00 AM when the Madrid-Ferrol Renfe train pulled into the station at Santiago de Compostela. A group of nearly 30 individuals massed in the south east corner of the station. Ieke Rollands stood in the center of the group looking not much different than a tour guide giving last minute instructions to a group of neophyte travelers.

He began speaking slowly. "Okay you sorry bunch of losers, we are here for one task and one task only. That task is to grab the Chereb and the Clavis and to get outta here. I do not care about anything else. We have a short walk to the hotel and very little time. We have a few hours until daybreak and I want to be gone by then. You have your instructions and plans. Let's split up and meet at the hotel in 30 minutes. Remember we leave no footprints, not a stone unturned. We are ghosts."

The group disbanded and moved out of the station toward the old town square. They had less than two miles to cover in order to reach the Hotel Paradores, the grand old palace where Jake, Sherry and the Old Man were sleeping.

The streets were nearly vacant as groups of two and three moved in toward the square and the old hotel. In the early morning darkness, the streets glimmered as dew covered the old stone walks. The plan called for a group of four to enter the building and slowly move in on Jake and Sherry.

Jake and Sherry were located on the third floor in a room facing the old Cathedral. There was one watchman on duty and he happened to be sitting in the corner of the main entry. He was smoking a cigarette. He did not notice the small groups of men who filed past and into the hall. There were no security cameras and the halls were vacant.

38

FIRE AND LIGHT

Sherry was awakened by what she thought was an old door slowly being opened on the outside balcony. As she recalled the details of the patio she concluded that the sound had come from a loose board. For a moment she held her breath, as she listened motionlessly. She also thought she heard a creak outside the door of the grand old room.

"Jake," she whispered, "Did you hear that?"

Jake did not move. She nudged him. "Jake I heard something on the balcony."

Sherry reached to her right and grasped the Chereb; she lay on the table the night before. Jake sat up in bed with his head cocked slightly to the right. He felt the blood course through his temples— pounding as he strained to hear whatever might be out of the ordinary. He thought he heard a chirp from a plank in the hall just outside the door.

He scampered out of the bed, as Sherry slid out of the other side. Jake motioned to her. She could barely make out his hand as the dim light from the street below meagerly cast its rays into the room, just inside the heavy curtain valance. Now, Jake was at the door and she stood at the curtain on the far side of the room. Jake watched in the dark, as the handle of the door moved slowly to the right. He pressed his back against the wall. He drew a breath ever so slowly. He heard his heart pounding and worried that it might be detected by others. Sherry stood stock still, as she faced the large drape covering the opening.

On the other side of the door where Jake stood were two men; one of whom inserted a small plastic wafer connected via a BUS and wire system to his personal computer. The computer, within seconds ran nearly a thousand combinations and then hit on the proper sequence. The small, fine-featured man, dressed in black was turning the knob. The other man had his hand on the handle of a dark metal object. The small man pushed the door open, no more than one inch. He waited, motionless. The two men were merely inches from Jake who was positioned just to the left of the door.

Jake squinted as he tried to detect any clues as the door swung ever so slowly. He held his breath. Within what to Jake seemed like minutes, the door began to move rapidly. Jake watched a hand and forearm move into the dimly lit room.

When the door was nearly half open Jake grabbed the arm and immediately twisted the hand in toward him. Now, he drove his forehead into the shoulder of the man. He seized and secured the other arm from behind as he pushed the man back into the hall. He heard the crash, as the hand-held computer bounced off the floor. He was now in full view of the second man, whose eyes were as big as saucers. Jake noticed that the eyes were locked on him. Jake heard yelling and wondered if it was he, or one of the other men. He did not have time to analyze.

He drove the man forward and was now forcing the guy into the other person. The slightly-built fellow was now brandishing a knife with a blade that reflected the dim light of the early hour. Jake steered his prey into the other, who was now slashing wildly, hitting nothing but air. As Jake and the first man crashed into the far wall the second man was moving backward toward the same wall.

For what seemed to Jake as no reason, the man with the knife turned and started running down the hall away from the action. As Jake now had the man in a choke hold, he began to drag him back toward the room he just moments earlier exited. Jake glanced down the corridor as the other would be attacker disappeared behind the exit door at the end of the hall.

Jake drug the now unconscious and limp intruder, back into the room as a woman, in a green robe peeked her head out from behind the door. Jake closed the door behind him. As he frisked the man he found a large knife and plastic fasteners in his pocket. Jake pulled a few of the ties out and secured the guy's feet and hands with the plastic cords.

Jake was now training his vision on the far side of the room. Sherry was not there. He ran to the window and noticed that the door leading outside was smashed. As he leapt onto the balcony he witnessed a strange blue light filling his view and a snapping sound crackling in his ears. Sherry was in the corner of the balcony with her hand in the air. He observed that the Chereb was in Sherry's raised hand.

A person in black was on the edge of the balcony screeching like a wild parrot. As Jake watched, the person suddenly exploded into a fog of shimmering, dust like particles. The fog seemed to fill the space. As it moved upward, it seemed to add more darkness to the early morning sky. At least, that is what Jake thought he saw. Sherry turned to Jake. Her eyes were like fire, almost piercing Jake's.

"Come on Jake we must go," she yelled as she offered her hand. She was now on the stone wall above the deck as she pulled him up.

How does she have the strength to do that? Jake wondered as he began to teeter on the top of the rail.

Without warning, Sherry leapt off the perch with Jake in tow. For Jake, time was racing at tortoise pace. As they arched toward the ground, Jake noticed Ieke Rollands and Kareem Razier on the square below. They were within a few steps. As he and Sherry touched the ground, Ieke raised his fist; a blue light was arching from his hand.

The blue current contained traces of yellow as the stream of light and heat raced toward Sherry's Clavis covered right wrist. Jake could feel the heat, as energy from Sherry's right hand exploded. Jake watched fire come out of her forearm. As Sherry and Jake reached the pavement Jake felt pulses of energy surging through his feet.

With a dagger in hand and fire in his eyes, Ieke lunged toward Sherry. Sherry saw his approach and stepped aside. As she did, out of nowhere Kareem dove at Ieke tackling him from behind. The two hit the ground hard and the Clavis on Ieke's wrist became dislodged, as his arm slammed against the ground. The Clavis rolled slowly toward Sherry, spewing sparks as it turned.

Jake and Sherry flew backwards and Jake landed somehow atop her shoulders. They rolled to a stop in a small twisted pile. Jake looked at his right leg. It twisted at an odd angle to the right. He knew in an instant that it was a compound fracture. A trickle of blood came from the spot where a small piece of his tibia was exposed. Before shock could set in he felt Sherry's hand touch the spot. To his utter amazement, as she released her grip the leg was straight and there was no evidence of the break. His joy was short lived; for as he stood up and turned his focus on Sherry he saw the truth.

As he looked down, he watched the life draining from Sherry's face she was growing cold. He yelled no, no, no! He turned away and was nearly blinded by the glowing cuff rolling across the stones toward them. Mysteriously, it ended up on Sherrie's wrist, like it was being directed there. As he watched, Sherry was transformed before his eyes. Her body began to glow. As it glowed it began to shimmer, like a diamond in the sunlight and yet somehow brighter and clearer.

She was standing with her arms raised in the air. She clasped the Chereb by the handle, in both hands. The air smelled of ozone, clean and pure. Jake instinctively grabbed Sherry's right-hand side and left arm. As he did he felt a pulse of energy and fell back. He looked down and his shoes were gone and he watched smoke come from his arms. He was dazed.

Ieke Rollands was pounding the ground as Jake struggled to stand. Kareem was on his knees with his head down. His hands clasped, fingers interlocked. Jake surveyed the area. He saw foggy smoke, coming from the street, where black-robed men once were. These clouds mingled with the other plumes already gathering. Sherry appeared to be transparent, as she hovered over the ground. She was moving slowly as she rose higher and became more translucent; yet her outline was clear and bright.

Jake yelled, "Stop please, stop!"

He was motoring in Sherry's direction. As he approached Sherry's voice thundered over the ground, "Ieke Rollands you are the least among us and you and your kind are like the cancer that ravages the body. You sneak in slowly at first, and then you steal the very essence of life from the very small parts. You are death. You are separate, not by my choice, but by your own carbon-black pride driven by glacier like greed."

As the word death came out of her mouth, Ieke Rollands burst to a dusting of dark ash. The smell of Sulphur and cedar smoke filled the air. The darkness spread. Kareem remained face to the ground. Jake turned his head earthward as he thought he saw the Old Man's brow furrowed, looking on from a distance of a hundred feet or so.

He saw what might have been a wind coming from Old Man's mouth. Jake began to feel a burning sensation in his wrists. He looked down and his feet were blistered. He was, for a brief instant, overcome with fear. With tears of pain and joy in his eyes, he saw Sherry. She motioned to him. He worked his way closer.

He heard her whisper, "Jake now you are eht naidraug dna eht trofmoc. Ours is to care for the weak and the abused and to water the truth and feed the vulnerable. You will not fail. The Chereb and Clavicularius are at your side and they are your shield."

"Sherry," Jake said, "I am not ready."

"You are ready, as you are able," she said.

Jake was transfixed as Sherry's image began to glow a bright white. As her likeness changed, streams of bright specs seemed to flow from her hands, feet and side.

"Please Sherry don't leave us we need you, I need—" he yelled.

"syawla uoy htiw ma I." Razier heard.

Jake looked up as the Chereb and the Cuffs seemed to slide through Sherry's arms and hands. As they did they were transformed into a large ball of fire. As Jake watched, the ball of fire exploded with the brilliance of a rainbow, as tiny multicolored particles spread across the entire sky.

They seemed to transform the dark clouds that moments earlier were the essence of Ieke and his men. As the particles combined the colors became brighter and lighter. These crystalline flecks of light spread out over the sky. They flickered as they floated to the ground. There was a silky glitter on the ground that seemed to extend on, as far as he could see. The ground not only flickered but it was as if the terrain was backlit with a golden-hued white light.

Through the mist and brilliant flickering light, Jake turned his gaze heavenward. He was still focused on, what moments earlier, was sweet Sherry, whom he knew and loved. Now the barely-visible image of Sherry slowly disappeared into the heavens surrounded by a veil of brilliant pure-white light. The sound of joyous music seemed to fill the air. He laughed. It was the sound of pure beauty. It was a wonder that shocked him to his bones.

39

SADNESS AND JOY

Razier was on his knees, face down and motionless. He was frightened, alarmed, and at the same time, he felt a peace and exhilaration. What he had seen and mostly heard, as he later recounted, defied description, in human words. Yet more importantly, he was a broken man. He was devastated, because, at that very moment he had come to realize that all that he had worked for, all that he had cared for and all that he had believed in, were wrong.

He was experiencing his own rebirth. Like the street he was now facing, he was living a Renaissance. It formed the main square; people were beginning to prepare for their daily duties. Along the circumference, carts filled with trinkets were slowly unwrapped from their canvas cocoons by local merchants. Shopkeepers were unrolling metal-clad shades from the windows they covered and old men were taking their places on familiar benches.

Jake was sitting on the edge of the large center fountain for what seemed to him, hours. He now studied the marks left in his hands, feet and side. They burned with pain and at the same time seemed to provide him comfort and connection to something great. He thought he saw them bleeding light. The sun was making its daily climb from the east as the light began to warm the cold and wet stones. They still shimmered in the emerging light.

Razier slowly lifted his head and spoke in halting words. "Jake, I have done horrible things in my life. I followed what I thought to be the right path, but I was wrong. I thought that Ieke was on the path of goodness. I now know that he was—, I mean, I was wrong. He was not responsible for what I have done; I am. The good is not found in the thoughts one has, it is in the life I lead. Sherry was right; she was the good one. I want to make amends and I want to do the right thing Jake. Do you understand?"

Just then a little girl in a tattered yellow and white dress ran up from behind one of the many merchant vans and asked, "Are you two alright?"

Jake looked up slowly and said, "We have never been better and how are you doing this beautiful day?"

"Just fine sir," she said, "can you see the sparkles on the ground? Today is better."

Razier nodded and smiled as the little angel skipped back to the little white van now nearly fully transformed to a complete linen shop.

Jake heard a small clear voice. He knew it immediately; the voice was that of Sherry.

"meeraK uoy evigrof I, od I." She said.

Jake was not sure where the voice was coming from. He looked around. She was not there. There was nobody there.

Jake replied, "I hear you but I can't see you. Where are you Sherry?"

Somehow Jake knew the answer to his own question. He had to ask anyway.

It was Kareem who answered, "She has gone to the mountain."

Jake made eye contact with Kareem. His eyes lightened and he nodded his head in agreement.

"Jake you know that we both are after the good. To me you are like Ruh al Qudus. You are the rush of a mighty wind. I thought because Ieke spoke so powerfully in his general's uniform and because he was a knight, that he was for real. Jake he was not. That is why I warned the Old Man in a letter about our plans. That is why I did not participate in the attack. That is why I want to help you. Jake, what happened to your hand and feet and why is there blood on your side?"

Jake removed his gaze from Kareem and did not answer. He looked across the square and thought he saw Sherry and the Old Man sitting on a bench. The Old Man was looking at him. He was slowly shaking his head in affirmation. They both had an inexplicable glow within their faces.

After a certain time, Jake looked back at Kareem Razier. He said, "I don't know what happened to my hands, feet and side, but I do believe what you tell me. That means we now have a job to do. You will take what we have learned of the Clavis Ohrel. I will take what I have learned of the Chereb and the Clavis Ariel. I will return to you shortly and you will go to the remains of the old Mosque, in south end of town, there you will find the proper instruction and direction. After you do, meet me at the airport. We are headed for DC.

A few days later, Jake and Kareem were sitting in a meeting in the office. The black walnut block sitting on the desk read,

Christian D. Poincy Attorney at Law. He and two others were there with Jake and Kareem.

"So I understand you have found the items we were after, correct?" Christian asked.

"Yes sir we did," Jake replied.

"When will you hand them over?" A large guy in a dress military suit demanded.

Jake turned to Kareem, smiled and said, "They are in safe keeping. I assure you."

Christian said, "Now Jake, we need these artifacts. You will need to hand them over."

Jake turned to Kareem as he smiled broadly. Jake and Kareem rose and walked to the door.

Turning back to the group Jake said. "They are there for the taking."

40

CHASING THE LIGHT

Jake and Kareem sat in the ticketing area of Reagan National. Not much of substance was said. Kareem finally broke the awkward silence with a simple question. "So where do we go from here?" He said.

Jake slowly turned his head and looked squarely at Kareem.

He replied, "Yeah, I know things are going to be very different for both of us. I think you can understand that Christian and the others are none too happy with us. How can we explain how three of the most important artifacts ever to reach mankind have disappeared literally into thin-air? Can you imagine if we tried to explain how Ieke exploded into a puff of smoke? I even have trouble with that myself and I saw it with my own eyes."

Kareem began to laugh hysterically, "What will people say when we tell them that Sherry turned into an angel and flew off right in front of us?"

"Well my friend, I suppose they might respond like your Turkish friends. They may laugh but I am sure they won't like the fact that you have decided to go to Italy and learn about Bernardone." Jake suggested.

"I still know there is one true God and that there will be a judgement day; so I think they will be okay with that as long as I speak of Allah."

"Well, my brother, I guess I had better get on my way. I am headed back to Arizona and I can't wait to see the kids. Be safe and keep in touch."

"I will and you take care too. There are people who are not happy at all. I have your back buddy."

"I understand; that's why I want to get out of here."

Both men stood and embraced like brothers. Jake headed toward the United counter and Kareem walked out of the main doors headed directly to the international terminal.

Five hours later Jake was headed northbound on highway 17, speeding home to Sedona. As he drove up the canyon he was focused on the beauty of the earth. The drive up the canyon reminded him of the life and family.

Shortly after he passed the Cherry Road exit, Jake saw a large boulder headed towards his windshield. He yanked the wheel to the right. Just as the two hundred pound boulder made contact the car swerved off the highway and slid down an embankment. He hit his head on the steering wheel. Jake lost consciousness.

Moments later, he was dragged from the car. He did not know who was dragging him. He thought he was awake as twisted free from his captors and sprinted away downhill. He thought he saw Christian and two others giving pursuit. He wasn't sure. He did not take time to analyze why he Christian would after him—he just ran. He charged straight down a draw. His pursuers were close behind. He leapt over a large stone and slid on his rear, down the ravine. He felt the shock of a blow to the head. He began to crawl in the direction of a small cave. At that moment he felt the sting of what he now recognized as rocks landing on his back and legs.

He collapsed into the ground, face first. He lifted up his head and as he did time slowed. He was traveling down a long tunnel of pure light. It was not frightening. It was warm and inviting. He saw Sherry and the Old Man standing in front of him. As he reached toward Sherry, she extended her arms toward his.

At that very instant he felt a blow to his chest and then he fell, slowly at first then gaining speed as he hit the ground with a thud. He looked up. He looked up through foggy eyes. He thought he saw Kareem Razier bending over him with two metal paddles in his hand. Jake wanted to speak to Kareem. He wanted to ask why he was in northern Arizona and why he had a defibrillator in his hands. But as he tried to speak, he exhaled a long and slow breath. Kareem called his name, but Jake did not answer.

Jake felt someone drag him to the cave not far from Montezuma's well. The person seemed to him to be wearing a glowing suit. Jake was put on a bed of juniper bows by this person in glowing robes. The highway was not a long way off. At least he thought he heard the sound of tires on pavement in the distance.

41

THE DEVASTATING CRASH

Katy Rader walked into the kitchen and sat down to breakfast at the glass-topped table in the townhouse in the village of Oak Creek just a few minutes from Sedona, Arizona. The locals called the area the village because it was a few miles east of the main visitor's area and was less "touristy". Pancakes and boiled eggs were already sitting on dishes and milk and orange juice were next to each plate. For Katy and Sam life was good and it was nice for their grandparents also. It had been years since Jake and Sherry visited.

They missed their dad but accepted that duty, at times overrides family. According to Christian, Jake and Sherry were living in a small town in Chile called Puerto Montt De Sur. In addition, Christian had forwarded to the family regular letters from Jake and Sherry. These letters had given exciting and sometimes frightening details, as to their wandering adventures. For example in a recent letter, Jake shared how a large male sea lion surfaced next to his boat and ended up eating fish Jake had caught right out of the boat. The family got a good chuckle out of the story.

Ieke was not the main focus; it was working on the behalf of the poor. While it had been years, the kids did not seem to mind that they were living thousands of miles from Jake and Sherry. After all, Katy was an adult and Sam was involved in a college in the high school program. This would give him a leg up after he graduated. He did not want to leave high school yet, because he would miss the tennis team where he was the captain.

Sam looked out over the red rocks, as a large sparkling weather front appeared over the spires.

He said, "Isn't it beautiful; it's raining glitter!"

On the TV, hanging on the kitchen wall, a commentator began to describe the phenomena of the "Chereb fog" crossing all borders of all nations. This and the others of similar configuration seemed to form like normal storm clouds but as they did, people engaged in behaviors different and somehow more caring than normal. Neighbors were more neighborly, friends were friendlier and gifts of various kinds somehow occurred more frequently. Yet, it was not just the behavior.

The landscape became even more beautiful. Trees shimmered with vivid colors and grasses shone as if they were being lit from within. The end of the report reminded everyone that from a scientific point of view, there was no reliable and complete evidence of such a thing. There were scientists however, that had done studies that showed the reality of the notion.

In one study at UCLA, a group of biochemists found that the material scraped from the ground in Sedona was in fact "living." At least it contained forty four chromosomes. There were twenty two that seemed to be human in origin and twenty two that seemed to be plant in nature. There were other molecules; some were inexplicable. These additional substances were not in the form of the two missing chromosomes. The study team to conclude that more information was needed in order to, "More fully assess the material." •

"However," the speaker said, "the many who witnessed the events are staunch in their belief that they have witnessed a miraculous reality."

"Do you ever wonder if Dad and Sherry are experiencing down in Chile, what we are seeing here?" Katy said as she picked up the boiled egg."

"You know they are with you in spirit. Your dad is committed to helping others and that is just the way it is." Grandma said in a less than convincing manner.

"Hey kids, it's a beautiful June day and we have booked a scenic helicopter tour of Sedona and the Grand Canyon for your eighteenth birthday Katy. How does that sound?" Gramps said.

After breakfast and a few objections from Sam the group headed down to the tour helicopter at the airport. After what seemed to Sam to be endless and somehow needless instructions, the fun began. The trip up to the canyon was spectacular. The red rocks glistened with a new mist in the early morning sun. As the helicopter wound its way up Oak Creek Canyon the water flowing over Slide Rock Park sparkled as it moved like liquid diamonds covering the slippery red rocks underneath.

Sam yelled, "Look, a rafting party," as a group of what looked like teenaged boys floated down the creek on old black inner tubes. Joy was in the air.

The tubing kids linking arms were hooked together in a line. From the copter they seemed to be ants as they bounced down the creek over the large smooth red limestone rocks.

As the chopper moved into a small handing fog bank, suddenly and without warning a large pop came from the engine behind the cabin. The helicopter began to spin uncontrollably down to the ground. Her stomach in her throat, Katy watched with focused eyes as the pilot frantically grabbed at the unresponsive controls. For a moment, the sound of the rotor blades was the only thing she heard.

First there was a sputter and then only the wisp of rotor blades turning in the air. Upward pressure could be felt as her legs were pressed into the seat below her buttocks. Then the roar of the engine was heard again. The helicopter began to right itself and turn toward uptown Sedona. For the moment the fear left the pilot's eyes.

Before anyone could take a breath the copter dove as there was no power. It began to spin on a path to the ground. Not Katy, Sam or anyone else said a word as the chopper twisted earthward. Katy felt the impact as the body of the craft smashed onto the rocks just to the left of the flowing creek water.

Katy felt a burst of heat from the burning craft. It surged forward, across her face and then receded. She slowly cleared her head and looked over at the pilot he was motionless. Katy had been thrown from the craft and was lying in a small pool of water nearly 60 feet from the fuel-fed fire that blazed on impact. The chopper was now a tin inferno. She yelled out. She tasted blood in her mouth and noticed that her arm was lying oddly as her forearm rested at a 90 degree angle to her wrist.

The tongues of fire rose then retreated in a slow-motion dance and then she passed out. On a ridge a few miles away a hiker saw what appeared to be a flash followed by a popping sound. Katy did not know that the cloud of grey smoke rising from the forest floor pinpointed the location of the crash.

After what must have been twenty minutes, Katy was awake and started to stand. She slipped on a rock and fell to the ground. As the light of the sun slowly slipped from the heart of the valley, Katy began to stumble along with the flow of the water. Dazed and confused she moved onward, away from what was now the burned and charred wreckage of the tour helicopter and all its hapless inhabitants. Katy did not look back as she moved down the creek. She did not remember her family. She wandered aimlessly down the hill.

There were no rescue vehicles, reporters, or gawkers. She did not hear the wail of the fire rescue vehicle that had been summoned by the dispatcher who had been called by the 911 operator. She did not know that the Sedona Airport Control Center had advised the EMT's and search and rescue that the chopper was "feared down."

Alone and frightened, Katy limped, staggered and lunged down the ever darker and colder Oak Creek. Katy, severely injured and traumatized, sometimes walked and often crawled as she continued downstream. She was driven by the inexplicable desire to live.

She managed to cover nearly two miles in her semiconscious condition. Less than two hundred yards from Katy's location, a small group of young adults sat around a campfire, in a small private campground not more than two miles from uptown Sedona. Clay Berry, a cub reporter from the Phoenix Sand newspaper, was sitting in his folding chair roasting his third hotdog over the open fire. He and four friends were enjoying a well-deserved day away from work, just a couple of hours north of Phoenix.

As he sat back in his chair attempting to get a glimpse of his freshly cooked masterpiece, a "dawg" cooked to perfection, over an open fire, he heard a sound coming from directly behind him. Startled, he stood up, knocking over a large bottle of water. As he looked in the direction of the sound, he made out the grizzly figure of a human form moving in his direction; not more than ten feet away. Shivers worked their

199

way down his spine as he felt his eyes and ears intensify their attention. A bear was the first thought that ran through his head. As he listened, he heard someone shout.

"It is a young woman." He heard coming from his own lips; yet, somehow the words seemed strangely different and somehow distant.

As he focused on the movement, he felt the others moving toward the creek and in the direction of what he recognized as a young woman, badly injured. With matted hair and blood stains covering her face, she looked like a zombie; not a beautiful eighteen year old girl.

Clay was first to reach her. She let out a frightful scream as he reached out to comfort her. She looked into his eyes. He could see a lifeless glaze. She collapsed into his arms.

Clay yelled, "Call nine, one, one," as he gradually lowered the young thing to the ground. He felt the anxiety as a friend in the background spoke in a high pitched tone. He spoke to the emergency operator, who could not understand. Clay slowly rubbed what was a snarled and matted mess of hair on the victim's head, as he waited for what seemed like hours. As he sat he could hear, faintly in the distance, the wail of the emergency siren. Starting out as a slight whisper, the sound gradually became so loud that he covered his ears. Then it stopped, just as the lights of the vehicle became visible. As it moved closer to their position he smiled. The sound of tires crunching small rocks filled Clay's ears as the medical truck came to a stop not more than ten feet away.

Within seconds a flurry of activity began as a female paramedic sprang from the passenger-side door. He felt bangs and bumps as he was pushed aside. The team of emergency personnel dislodged Katy from his arms and flopped her on the gurney.

"Blood pressure eighty over forty," the paramedic yelled.

"Pulse slow and irregular," was the next thing out of the paramedic's mouth.

"Breathing is shallow and staccato-like." The paramedic yelled.

The driver of the emergency vehicle arrived moments after the paramedic who had been taking the blood pressure measurements.

He said, "I have a compound fracture of the right forearm. It appears to be the right radius. About three inches down from the ulna."

He shined a light into the young girl's eyes.

"Right eye fixed and dilated," he said. "Left eye is within normal limits. There does not appear to be any back injuries," he said to the other paramedic, as they slowly turned her over to her side.

Clay got up and made his way through the group of people as an ambulance arrived at the scene. The two ambulance workers jumped out of the white and orange ambulance. The driver opened the rear door and began to pull the chrome and white stretcher from the rear of the vehicle. As he pulled, the wheels automatically lowered to ground-level. The ambulance workers rolled the stretcher bed over the uneven and bumpy ground to the young girl.

Clay strained to watch as the girl was fastened to the stretcher bed and rolled to the back of the ambulance. As she was pushed into the vehicle the paramedic and the ambulance assistant jumped inside also. On impulse, Clay jumped into the ambulance reaching out for Katy's hand.

"You're her brother?" the paramedic asked as the ambulance pulled out of the campground. Clay said nothing. Unnoticed by anyone, Jake and Sherry looked on knowing that they shouldn't do anything more.

42

THE COVER STORY

According to a letter written by Christian Poincy, Jake and Sherry had been living in the small town of Puerto Montt, Chile. While things generally had been good, there were ups and downs, as there are in any marriage. Jake admitted that he lost patience with Sherry from time to time. According to Sherry, Jake shed regular tears as he talked with joy about his kids and the life he had sacrificed in order to neutralize Ieke Rollands and his devastating quest. Jake and Sherry loved helping people, especially locals. The reason they stayed at the far end of the South American continent was Ieke. He was said to have been training a group of anarchists in the area.

Christian confirmed that Ieke Rollands had a long history, while not totally documented, of unsavory activities including suspicions that he was behind the killing of students at the University of Texas during the 1970's. Most recently, a member of a terrorist group of radical Islamists had implicated him in the dramatic and much publicized incident in Seattle, Washington. Sherry was taken and held hostage by members of Rollands' radicalized ranks.

While an indictment was issued, years earlier, there was only sketchy information as to his whereabouts. Because Jake and Sherry were members of a small group of secret agents called the Knights of St. John, they were given the mission to seek out Rollands and bring him to justice. This fact was confirmed in a personal conversation Clay had with Christian Poincy.

After years of near misses, Christian believed that they were getting closer to Rollands and his small band of thugs. But these facts were only confirmed in letters. Katy had stated that she doubted that the letters were penned by Jake. She did not however, know who might be ghostwriting the items.

The frequently-reported and well-documented "Chereb fog," as it was called seemed to be spreading the world over. As it spread, violent crime, road rage and domestic disturbance decreased dramatically. Scientists, at this moment attempt to verify the properties of this strange and beautiful atmospheric disturbance which appeared suddenly in a small region of Spain. It was this very same region that Kareem Razier said his life was changed forever. He now lives on an island on a lake not far from Assisi, Italy. He confirmed that he, too, learned much from Francisco Bernardone.

Kareem says that Jake and Sherry are often in Arizona. He confirms that they look on as Clay is eating lunch in a small café in the hospital in Cottonwood, Arizona as he supports Katy in recovery. He spends his days pouring over letters and material provided to him by Katy. She is due to be released today. Clay continues to write feverishly as he sees a bigger story than the articles he has already written. Katy is sitting next to him.

Clay turns to Katy and says, "Did you know that scientists have analyzed the "Chereb fog." You know the beautiful sparkles that appear from time to time? They have discovered that the mist is made up of tiny particles. These particles seem to be a life form of sorts. They contain Deoxyribonucleic Acid. Not in a normal life sense, but like half. There are forty four chromosomes, but not in pairs. These particles also contain Hydrogen, Oxygen and Nitrogen. They seem to house various metals. But what is really weird is that they seem to be like tiny generators, producing warmth and light. They don't seem to degrade."

Katy looks at him with a blank stare. "All I know is that when the fog appears I feel better and closer to my family, ya know? That is all I need to know. It makes me warm inside like when my dad would hug me and tell me he loved me so much. That was just before they left."

Jake reaches out to touch Katy. He caresses her hair ever so gently. Jake sees her head move slightly in the direction of his caress. She does not respond in any other way. A small tear makes its way down Jake's face. He is happier than he has ever been and that is why he cries. Katy turns around and looks behind her as if she feels someone's presence. She knows someone is there but she actually sees no one. Clay is taking notes as he looks up from a letter written in Italy. He continues to try to make sense of the bizarre story that he pieces together from the letters written by Jake to his dad; in addition to the others he received from Katy who swears Christian Poincy gave them to her in Washington DC. The problem he faces s that the story he put together from Christian is so very different from the letters Jake's dad left behind.

Why, he wonders, do Jake's and Christian's letters differ so much?

Jake and Sherry are there right beside Clay and Katy. They speak but all too often, nobody seems to be listening.

Jake turns to Sherry and says, "Emit erom tib a deen tsuj, emit meht evig."

Clay Berry continues to write for the paper and his series of articles are popular reading for a generation of people who search for the truth. Jake, Sherry and the Old Man are well and according to Kareem are watching and protecting Katy and Clay. In fact, Kareem is the one who stated that Jake and Sherry were in the hospital with Clay and Katy. Frankly, many see these and other irrational ramblings, as the utterances of an old and troubled soul.

Clay tracked down Kareem on a trip to Italy. According to Clay, Kareem lives as a 'hermit' working as a consultant, friend and advocate for those who are sick and unfortunate. He has a constant and compelling smile. He assured Clay that Jake and Sherry communicate with him regularly, but nobody had seen them. He lives a simple life in a small shack in a tiny village.

Most of his time is spent in Mosques, Temples and Churches explaining the essential values of hope, humility and love. He generally says little of the Chereb and the Clavicularius except that they were truly the source of his joy. He insists that they are there for anyone who dares to search for them. He often points to the earth and to the rainbows that seem to appear ever more frequently above. Clay insists that Kareem confirmed much of what was written about Jake, Sherry, Ieke Rollands and the Old Man.

"I can tell clearly that Clay believes the story and I have done what I can to tell you the facts as I know them. By the way, according to Kareem Razier, Jake's parents and Sam are constantly there alongside Jake and Sherry, yet, he has not said how he knows this to be true." Ann said.

"He just knows!" Ruth exclaimed

"Yes and as for Rollands and his minions; who knows? As I told you earlier, I am Clay's editor at the paper and I have been a witness to the documents and background information Clay used in his stories. I have to admit, Jake, Sherry and the Old Man have changed my life. I feel that I actually know them. Some of the material seems miraculous and to some improbable, but that is what makes life so interesting and exciting does it not?" Ann said to Ruth.

The stewardess said, "Sorry to interrupt but all the other passengers have left the plane and the cleaning crew is here."

As Ann stood to leave, Ruth took one last look out of the small cabin window. Her eyes were drawn heavenward. She noticed the likenesses of human images forming in the clouds. As she looked closer she thought she observed the Maestro looking on as Jake, Sherry and Jake's family were together. Behind them was the Old Man arm in arm with Paulo and Cephas. A mist began to fall as she saw Francisco Bernardone in the distance. A tear ran down her cheek. She rubbed her eyes, shook her head and wondered if in fact she had been dreaming.

Made in the USA
San Bernardino, CA
25 June 2017